BartLett
and the
City of
fLames

Text copyright © 1999 by Odo Hirsch
Illustrations © 1999 by Andrew McLean

Published by Bloomsbury, New York and London
Distributed to the trade by Holtzbrinck Publishers
Library of Congress Cataloging-in-Publication Data
Hirsch, Odo.
Bartlett and the city of flames / by Odo Hirsch;
[illustrations by Andrew McLean].
1st U.S. ed. p. cm.
Sequel to: Bartlett and the ice voyage.
Summary: When the Pasha of the City of Sun becomes convinced that
Gozo is his kidnapped son, Bartlett and Jacques le Grand try to rescue their
young friend by using "Ingenuity, Perseverance and Desperation" to get the
Pasha's real son back from the underground City of Flames.
ISBN 1-58234-831-6 (alk. paper)
[1. Adventure and adventurers--Fiction. 2. Kidnapping--Fiction.]
I. McLean, Andrew, 1946- ill. II. Title.
PZ7.H59793 Bao 2003
[Fic]--dc22
2003051864

First U.S. Edition 2003
1 3 5 7 9 10 8 6 4 2

Bloomsbury USA Children's Books
175 Fifth Avenue
New York, New York 10010

ABOUT THE AUTHOR

ODO HIRSCH'S books for children include *Bartlett and the Ice Voyage*, *Bartlett and the City of Flames*, *Hazel Green* and *Antonio S and the Mystery of Theodore Guzman*.

His first book, *Antonio S and the Mystery of Theodore Guzman*, was immediately popular with children and adults. It was short-listed for the 1998 National Children's Literature Award in the Festival Awards for Literature, was an Honour Book in the 1998 Children's Book Council of Australia Book of the Year Awards, and won the inaugural Patricia Wrightson Prize for Children's Literature in the 1999 NSW Premier's Literary Awards.

Odo Hirsch was born in Australia where he studied medicine and worked as a doctor. He now lives in London. His books have been translated into several languages.

BartLett
and the
City of
fLames

by Odo Hirsch

BLOOMSBURY

Chapter 1

A full moon rose in the sky. In valleys of rock, moonlight broke against edges of stone and fell across boulders. Shadows lay like bottomless lakes. The silence was darker than the night itself.

In one of the valleys, two guardsmen lay asleep.

Their heads rested on rocks. Their cloaks, drawn up to their chins, were their only protection from the cold. Yet they slept. Their eyes did not see the moon as it followed its course in the sky above them.

The moon disappeared. In the hour before dawn, the darkness was thick. Dew came, and left its film over the guardsmen. Now a tide of light seeped faintly into the sky. Now the east brightened.

The sun burst over the horizon and released a flood of light.

One of the guardsmen awoke. He frowned, blinking, then stared at a small pebble that lay in front of his nose, as if that particular pebble could explain to him why he had just awoken with his head on a rock in a cold valley with the dawn breaking in the sky above him. But the pebble didn't explain anything, and even if it had been *able* to do so, and had been *willing* to do so, it probably wouldn't have found anything unusual in the situation, because, after all, the pebble lay there every day, in exactly the same place, and would probably continue to do so for years to come.

The guardsman brushed it away.

He sat up. His name was Bargus.

'Wake up!' he called out to his companion. Bargus disliked being the only one awake. The other guardsman was called More, which, everyone agreed, was a ridiculous name for anyone to have, and so no one would let him change it. 'More's enough and you don't deserve more, More,' people were fond of saying, without stopping to think whether More was fond of hearing it.

'Wake up, More,' called Bargus again, and this time he reached across and shoved More's shoulder.

More rolled over and opened his eyes. For a moment he stared at Bargus' face as if it were a pebble. Then he realised that the only reason he could see Bargus' face was because it was light, and if it was light . . . it must be day, and if it was day . . . it must be time to get up . . .

More groaned.

Bargus stood. He pulled his cloak around him, shivering. He stamped his feet. Here in the stonefields, the days shimmered in a haze of heat and the nights froze under an icy moon. By noon it would be like a furnace, but dawn always broke with a dense chill that found its way down every nerve and vein of your body.

The stonefields were a vast place of rock and boulder. Nothing grew there, except for tiny fingers of moss which lodged deep in crevices of the stone. The rock was red or pink, the colour of rust, and of blood, the colour of roses, and everywhere you walked there were pebbles and plates of stone slipping under your feet. There were no trees, but columns of rock rose above the ground. Some were crooked, some were straight, some twisted like corkscrews, some were jagged like slivers of broken glass, and some looked like people who had stood too long in one place and had been turned into stone by the cold of the night.

Bargus and More had camped in the shelter of a hill. Not far away a stone column rose into the air, thin at each end and fat in the middle, as if it had something inside it, like a snake that had just swallowed a mouse.

More got up slowly. Bargus began to get impatient. There was really nothing to get impatient about, because there was nothing for them to do but walk over the stones all day, and the sooner they started walking, the further they would have to go. And yet that was what Bargus was like: he was always *going* somewhere, or wanting to go somewhere, and waiting was worse than doing, even when there was nothing very pleasant to do.

'Have we got any bread left, More?'

More was still yawning and rubbing his eyes.

'Let me know when you find out,' said Bargus, and he walked away and began to climb the hill.

More opened his shoulder pack. Bargus always climbed hills—as soon as he saw one, he would run towards it. Only from the top of a hill, Bargus would say, could you see what was going on. And what ever *went* on? That was what More would have liked to know. All across the stonefields other guards were walking in pairs, just like them, looking for people who never appeared, guarding against enemies who were never glimpsed. What was the point? They never saw anyone, never found anything. Why couldn't they walk some-where more pleasant, like the bazaar at home, for instance, or near the lovely cool lakes to the north? No. Day after day they had to march through the fields of rock. And climbing the hills was the worst of it. The stones always gave way under your feet, and half the time you tumbled back to where you had started. Why couldn't they at least stay in the valleys? And why couldn't they get up later, for that matter, and stop for a sleep in the middle of the day, if it came to that . . .

More looked to see where Bargus had gone.

Bargus was near the top of the hill, waving his arms to get his attention and tell him to come.

More rummaged in his pack. 'He could have looked for the bread himself,' he mumbled. If there was none left they would be back to hard biscuits that tasted like iron. No, he found some. He held it up for Bargus to see.

Bargus shook his head, but he continued to beckon, waving his arms more and more urgently. Suddenly he jumped up, looked over the top of the hill, crouched down, and beckoned to More again.

More stood up with the bread. Behind him, the stone column with the swollen belly gleamed red in the sunlight. He started climbing the hill. The stones slipped under More's feet. He moved carefully. He looked up and saw Bargus gazing at him, his eyes bulging with impatience.

'You should have taken some before if you were so hungry,' he said, holding out the bread when he reached him.

'I'm not hungry,' said Bargus in a fierce whisper, although he grabbed the bread and took a big bite of it. The crumbs flew out of his mouth. 'And keep your voice down. Have a look over the top.'

More frowned.

'Go on.'

Hesitantly, More looked over the top of the hill. An instant later he was crouching next to Bargus again.

'Who are they?'

'I don't know,' said Bargus.

Cautiously, they put their heads over the top of the hill again, and stared.

'Where did they come from?'

'Where do you think?' said Bargus, and there was a mixture of fear and excitement in his voice.

Before them lay a valley of stone, like the one in which they had spent the night, like all the valleys in the stonefields. Columns of rock grew out of the ground and studded the valley without pattern or order. There were clusters of boulders. On the other side was another hill. A long jagged crevice opened in it like a dark wound. That wasn't unusual, there were plenty of cracks and crevices in the hills of the stonefields.

No, it wasn't the hill that made them stare, or the

crevice that opened in its side. It was the fact that three people were standing in front of it.

Bargus poked More in the ribs. More jumped.

'I said, we'll need our spears,' Bargus whispered.

'I left them with our packs.'

'Well, go and get them.'

More looked at Bargus in alarm. 'You know,' he whispered, 'no one knows we've climbed this hill, Bargus. No one knows we've seen anything.'

'So?'

'Well, we could always . . . just . . . go down again . . . and . . . pretend . . .'

Bargus was gazing harshly at More.

'It was just . . . an idea. Just a thought, really.'

But Bargus was already staring across the valley again. 'The spears, More. Get them. Quickly!'

More nodded. He began to slip and slide his way down the hill. Bargus glanced over his shoulder for a moment to watch him go. Then he turned back to the look at the strangers on the other side of the valley.

'Pretend we didn't see them?' he muttered to himself, shaking his head. 'Ignore the best stroke of luck I ever had? No, after this, everything is going to change. This is going to be the best day of my life. All I have to do is *catch* them!'

Chapter 2

Rock!

Bartlett looked around.

Nothing but rock!

He was blinking, shading his eyes, trying to keep them open. But they had become accustomed to the shadows and darkness of caves. The light of the rising sun stabbed them with its brightness.

'Rocks!' shouted Gozo excitedly beside him. 'Everywhere! Where are we, Mr Bartlett?'

Bartlett didn't reply. He was thin and stringly, with a freckled face and strong, knobbly fingers. Gozo, with hair that stood up in spikes and a little, upturned nose, was barely more than a boy.

The third person who had come out of the cave, Jacques le Grand, was tall and broad, with powerful shoulders and curly black hair. He was still shading his eyes and getting used to the light. Bartlett glanced at him. Jacques shook his head. He didn't know where they were any more than Bartlett did.

Rock. Red rock.

'Like the valleys of Qrum,' said Bartlett.

Jacques shrugged. They were half a world away from Qrum, and even Qrum was not as bare, as harsh, as . . . *stony* as this.

They stood in front of the opening of the cave, gazing

at the valley, its strange crop of stone stalks, its boulders, and the pink hill that rose in the distance.

It was almost a year since the two explorers, Bartlett and Jacques le Grand, had delivered to the Queen the wonderful fruit called a melidrop that she had never before tasted. They had travelled half way across the world on an ice voyage in order to succeed, and it had turned out to be one of the most extraordinary, exceptional and exhilarating of their adventures. It was during this journey that they had met Gozo, who drove a wagon with melidrops from his uncle's farm each day.

He hardly looked old enough to be driving a wagon, hardly old enough to scamper aboard their ship, the *Fortune Bey*, and demand to go with them to find out what it was like to be an explorer. But that was what he did. And he refused to go home again when they had delivered the melidrop to the Queen. He had joined them after they had already come back from the frozen seas, which was the really dangerous, desperate part of the ice voyage. No, how could he decide if he wanted to be an explorer if he hadn't even been on a real adventure? Besides, he knew what they were going to do next: explore the Margoulis Caverns, the longest, deepest chain of caves in the world!

The Margoulis Caverns turned out to be longer and deeper than anyone had imagined. They had been underground for months. They had travelled hundreds of miles, south and east, following the caves, up and down, marching through vast echoing chambers where the roof disappeared into blackness above the flickering light of their candles, crawling through crevices where the rock clawed at their arms and legs. They had been up to their necks in icy water, up to their armpits in mud. Sometimes the darkness was so dense that their candles were barely able to push the shadows away from their faces. Sometimes gold had glittered in the walls where the candlelight fell, and sometimes diamonds sparkled, and they had seen all the colours of the earth, the glint of silver, the green of copper, the blood of iron, the grey of coal, the blue of sapphire, and crystals of purple, orange, yellow, lilac, pink, magenta and aqua that studded the rock where fire and pressure had created them millions of years before. There had been stalactites and stalagmites, like bare fangs in a gigantic jaw, and there had been real jaws as well, and bones of animals that had perished long ago, and human bones lying in bleak despair where they had fallen. Gozo yelped in fright the first time he saw a skull. Yet they were not discouraged, and every day they walked further, deeper into the caves, with the Inventiveness, Desperation and Perserverance that are the tools of true explorers.

And all of it they mapped. In the candlelight, each time before they slept, Bartlett traced the path that they had followed, the distances, the chambers, and wrote what they had found there. Eventually the map covered fifteen scrolls of paper, and they were wrapped carefully in waterproof leather, and stored in a sack that Jacques le Grand carried under his arm.

And then they found that they were walking upwards. The caves grew drier. They began to find bones again, as if they were nearing an opening through which animals could enter. Then one time they settled down to sleep in the darkness—they no longer knew whether it was night or day, because the movement of the sun meant nothing here in the depths of the earth, and it was their weariness that measured time for them—and when they opened their eyes they saw something they had not seen for months: sunlight!

It was morning sunlight that had woken them, pouring through a crevice in the rock. They had flopped down with weariness during the night, not knowing that the end of the Margoulis Caverns was barely more than a stone's throw away.

So they followed the light to the opening, and stepped outside into a world of red stone.

Gozo kicked a pebble. It bounced away and hit a big rock. His skin was pale after all those months underground. And he had grown, of course, since that day, almost a year earlier, when he had leapt onto the deck of the ship called the *Fortune Bey*. Yet he still didn't look old enough to be exploring in a valley of rock, and he still shouted excitedly when anything surprised him.

'There's no one else here, Mr Bartlett,' he said, in case Bartlett hadn't noticed.

Bartlett had noticed.

'And it doesn't really look as if there's likely to be anyone along soon. It looks quite . . .' Gozo gazed at the valley.

'Empty?'

'That's right. I would have thought of it if you'd given me a minute.'

Jacques le Grand raised an eyebrow. Gozo was always thinking of things he would have thought of if someone had given him another minute. But this morning, Jacques didn't let it annoy him. He raised his face to the sky, closed his eyes and breathed in deeply. Sun! Beautiful, beautiful sun!

'Come on, let's go,' said Bartlett.

'Where to?' asked Gozo.

'Anywhere. Over there, for instance,' said Bartlett, pointing to the hill on the other side of the valley. 'An explorer, Gozo, never stays still. Not unless he's lost and he knows there's someone coming to get him. And there's no one coming to get *us*, is there?'

'No, Mr Bartlett.'

'And we're not lost, are we?'

Gozo hesitated, glancing doubtfully around him.

'We just don't know where we are,' said Jacques le Grand, grinning.

'Exactly,' said Bartlett. 'And not knowing where you are isn't the same as being lost. I could name a hundred differences . . .'

Gozo waited.

'But we haven't got time. Come on, let's go.'

Gozo turned back to the opening in the rock. It was hard to believe he had spent all that time underground, and this was the end.

'Goodbye, caves,' he murmured.

'Goodbye, Gozo.'

Gozo jumped. Caves couldn't talk! But it was Bartlett who had called out over his shoulder. It really *would* be goodbye if Gozo didn't hurry, because Bartlett and Jacques had set off without so much as a glance back-wards, and they were already striding away.

Gozo ran after them, scrambling over the sliding stones.

They marched off across the valley, passing the columns of rock which grew in this strange landscape instead of trees. There was not a soul to be seen, not a dog, not a bird, not a caterpillar. But Jacques couldn't keep the smile off his face. Every breath he took was as sweet as perfume. The sun was warm, the air was fresh. There was nothing above him but sky, the blue, blue sky that he had not seen for so long. What could possibly spoil it?

Two men, suddenly stepping out from behind a big clump of boulders, with spears in their hands. *That* could spoil it!

Chapter 3

Bargus raised his spear. The three strangers were pale. *Pale as the Moon.* He looked around for More. More was standing just behind him. More could have come a little further forward, Bargus thought, there was plenty of room.

'Hello.'

Bargus frowned. Hello? It was the one in front who had spoken.

'Hello,' said Bartlett again.

'Hello,' said More.

'Be quiet!' Bargus hissed at him. This wasn't the time to strike up a conversation. This wasn't the time for friendly 'hellos' and pats on the back. This was the time for something else altogether!

Bargus gazed at the strangers again, sizing them up. The one who had spoken was thin and stringly, but there could be surprising strength in stringly arms, Bargus knew. And then there was the other one, the broad-chested giant, whose arms looked powerful enough to knock a spear right out of your hand and whose fists looked big enough to drive you halfway into the ground if he decided to thump you on the head. Bargus gripped his spear tightly. Capturing them had seemed much simpler from the other side of the valley. *Surprise them . . . Point your spear . . . And . . .* He hadn't really stopped to think about what was meant to come next.

But now everyone seemed to be waiting for him to do something.

Bargus took a deep breath. 'You're our prisoners.'

Bartlett grinned. 'Your prisoners? I don't think so.'

'Yes you are. See?' Bargus thrust his spear forward fiercely, to show them what he meant.

Bartlett shook his head. 'No, you really are mistaken. Look.' Bartlett hopped quickly to the left. The two guardsmen jumped in fright. Bartlett hopped smartly to the right. 'You see, if I was your prisoner, I wouldn't be able to do that. I wouldn't be able to do anything you didn't tell me to do, would I?'

'No,' said More.

'More!'

'It's true, Bargus. He's right. He isn't our prisoner, and neither are the others. I bet they could all hop if they wanted to and I don't think we could stop them.'

'They're from the *Underground*, More,' Bargus hissed again, hoping the strangers couldn't hear him. 'We have to take them prisoner.'

'Why?' demanded Bartlett. 'You don't have to take us prisoner. Lots of people go underground. How else are you meant to explore a cave?'

Bargus didn't reply. He was too busy to answer questions. First there was More who wanted everyone to start hopping, and then there was . . . there was the big stranger, who hadn't taken his eyes off him for an instant. A shiver of fear ran down Bargus' spine.

Jacques le Grand gazed at Bargus steadily. To Jacques, it didn't look like these two guardsmen had ever used their spears against a rabbit, much less a person. In the space of three seconds, with one fast leap and a thrust of the arm, he'd bet he could sweep aside the spear of the first guard and have him pinned to the ground beneath him, and as for the second, he'd run away as fast as his legs could carry him. Even Gozo would frighten him off!

But Jacques didn't leap. He was thinking exactly the same thing as Bartlett: they couldn't take the risk. If both the guards managed to run away, they would be back to where they started, stranded in a valley of rock with no idea where they were. In fact, meeting the guards was the best thing that could have happened to them—only it was important that *they* didn't realise it.

Bartlett took a step closer to the guards. 'You could *try* to take us prisoner. But we'd have to fight.'

'Let's fight, Mr Bartlett!' cried Gozo excitedly.

'We don't want to do that,' Bartlett continued, talking to Bargus. '*You* don't want to do that. Gozo here can be very mean.' Bartlett leaned forward, lowering his voice. 'He bites.'

'I do not!'

Bargus glanced nervously at More. More didn't want to be bitten. And he didn't want the tall one to thump him on the head with his great clenched fist.

'Of course, we would be prepared to go with you . . .'

'Where to?' asked More.

'*More!*' cried Bargus. 'To the Pasha, of course.'

'Exactly,' said Bartlett, 'to the Pasha. But not as prisoners. As guests.'

'Guests?' repeated Bargus. The word almost made him sick. What would everyone think? Guardsmen didn't bring back *guests* from the Underground. They brought back prisoners . . . captives . . . hostages. They tied them up . . . blindfolded them . . . dragged them. At least, that was what Bargus had heard, because he had never actually captured anyone from the Underground before . . . or even seen anyone from the Underground . . . or even met anyone who had. But that only made it worse! *Everyone* would be watching. Everyone would come out to see. It was meant to be his triumph. And instead of hobbling into the city handcuffed, shackled, blindfolded as prisoners, they would be walking freely, talking happily, perhaps even singing a song . . . as guests.

Well, thought Bargus, we'll see about that! But what he saw was Jacques, the gigantic stranger with the huge clenched fists, still watching him closely, carefully, as if he could see exactly what he was thinking.

Bargus shivered and gripped his spear tightly.

Who was the Pasha? Where was his city? And why, why this fear of people who had been underground? Why this dread? Because Bargus did dread them, you could see it in the way he looked at them, the way he shivered when Jacques caught his eye, the way he kept his distance, held his spear, always at the ready. Bartlett didn't understand. More might easily have told them, but each time Bartlett tried to speak with him, More could barely get a word out before Bargus jumped in to silence him. Then Bargus would whisper urgently in his ear, and raise his fist, and shake his spear, and More would turn away and keep his silence.

For three days they marched through the red fields of stone, sharing the guardsmen's food and water, stopping once at a water hole in the bare rock. On the fourth day the rock gave way to sands, and then to a light soil, on which grew thin grasses and low, gnarled trees, and sometimes they saw herds of goats tended by distant

goatherds. On the sixth day they came to a dirt road, and now there were clusters of tents in the fields beside it, and sometimes there were inns. People came out to see who was passing, and each time Bargus had only to raise his spear and roar 'From the Underground!' and the people stopped in their tracks, mothers clutched their babies, and there was fear and fascination on their faces.

As they passed they heard people whisper. 'Pale as the Moon! Pale as the Moon!' There was something here that Bartlett did not understand, something deep and powerful. Jacques shook his head. Gozo frowned, but there was no answer that Bartlett could give him. And if there was such fear of them here, what would happen to them when they came to the Pasha's city?

They walked. Mile after mile, beside the road. And on the tenth day they arrived.

When they first saw it, from a hill, it seemed that the earth itself was ablaze. The city shimmered in a glare of light. Its walls, its buildings were made of bright white stone, and threw back every beam of sunlight that hit them.

Bargus grinned. 'The City of Sun,' he cried proudly.

But they had barely a moment more to look at it, before Bargus was prodding them with the end of his spear. His manner became rougher, more hostile. He waved his spear menacingly as they marched. It was as if he were putting on a show for others who were watching.

They stopped before the city walls. The glare of sun-light reflected from the white stone was almost unbear-able. Only a single dark gate relieved the brightness. Bargus raised his spear high into the air.

'Prisoners,' he shouted. 'Prisoners from the Under-ground!'

'Guests . . .' Jacques growled. But this time Bargus ignored him. They were no longer guests, and you only had to look at what was happening in front of them to see that it was true.

A thousand faces had appeared on top of the walls. The doors of the city gate were drawing back, and a thousand guardsmen were pouring through it, not even waiting for the gate to open fully, as if even that much delay would be too much.

And now they were racing across the ground, spears raised, eyes burning fiercely, and a terrible din rose into the air as they roared towards them.

'Prisoners! Prisoners from the Underground!' cried Bargus' voice, over and over.

The flood of guardsmen rushed towards them. Bartlett and Jacques linked arms around Gozo's shoulders. Their muscles tensed, their wrists tightened. Three abreast, with Gozo in the middle, they waited for the onslaught to arrive.

Jostled, prodded, pushed, they were swept into the city. The flood roared around them. Bargus was high in the air, lifted triumphantly on shoulders of other guardsmen. More was somewhere behind them. They passed through the gate. Now they were in streets, alleys. They came into a square and the torrent surged on and carried them across it. Balconies rose above them, faces peered down. Noise, colour. White walls, iron balconies, flashing eyes. Three abreast, arms straining to stay together, feet scrabbling for the ground, ears deafened. There was no time to look, to see. Blur. Bodies pressing and crushing them. A boiling river bouncing and plunging them in its current.

And then they stopped. There was noise—and then there was silence.

They were in a broad street. The crowd of guardsmen was still close around them. They saw Bargus, on his feet now, in front of a gateway in a high wall. The gate was closed. Its huge door was made out of solid planks and shining brass bolts.

Suddenly a small door, cut into the gate, opened. Out stepped a wonderfully dressed guard. His orange uniform glistened in the sunlight, and the feather in his turban shimmered now green, now blue as the light struck it. A curved dagger glinted in his belt.

'Prisoners,' Bargus stammered, his throat suddenly dry. 'Pris . . . prisoners from the Underground!'

The guard glanced at him disbelievingly. Then his eyes widened as he looked at the strangers. When he saw Gozo his eyes almost popped out of his head.

'I must tell the Pasha!'

'Yes, the Pasha!' The guardsmen were shouting again. 'The Pasha!'

'Six of you—no more—bring them in.'

Bargus stepped forward. Fifty others lunged for the gate. The foremost fought the others away, and, together with Bargus, took the prisoners inside. The door closed. Where was More? He had been left behind.

They were in a courtyard. The white stone dazzled the eyes.

The orange guard crossed the courtyard and disappeared. Time passed. From outside, the murmuring and shouts of the crowd could be heard.

'Now you'll see,' said Bargus, smirking at Bartlett. 'Now you'll see what it is to be a prisoner of the Pasha. He'll flay you, he'll turn you inside out, he'll . . .'

'Inside out?' said Bartlett. 'Really, Bargus!'

'He'll . . . I don't know *what* he'll do!' spluttered Bargus, trying to imagine what tortures the Pasha could think of. And it was true, the Pasha really did do something that neither Bargus nor anyone else would have predicted. Because when he finally arrived, bustling across the courtyard with twenty guards running to keep up, he stopped, took one look at Gozo . . . and fainted!

Chapter 4

The Pasha stroked his chin. He was sitting on his throne, wearing white silk robes that flowed around him all the way to the floor. Beside him, on a second throne, sat his wife, the Pashanne, and occasionally, as he stroked his chin, he glanced at her to see what she was thinking. But the Pashanne didn't glance back. She was gazing elsewhere, with great concentration, barely blinking her beautiful green eyes.

The throne room had tall windows. Sunlight streamed on to the blue and white tiles of the floor. The ceiling was a plaster masterpiece of swooping, swirling shapes. On the back wall was a vast mirror. The mirror was said to be the most perfect glass ever made, reflecting every image without the slightest flaw. The Pasha used it so he could see what was going on behind his courtiers as well as in front of them, and if anyone tried to whisper behind his hand, the Pasha was sure to spot it. He had a terrible temper and he often threw out four, five or six courtiers in a session, not letting them come back until they brought gifts of pomegranates and honeycomb.

It was a long way to the back wall. The throne room was enormous, easily big enough for three hundred people—five hundred, if everyone didn't mind squeezing together—and it was used for ceremonies,

announcements and other occasions when the Pasha
wanted to appear in all his splendour. But now it was
almost empty. There were only eleven people in it: the
Pasha and the Pashanne, attended by two guards in fabulous orange uniforms, the Conductor of Ceremonies,
who stood beside them, and Bartlett and Jacques le
Grand, surrounded by four guards who had brought
them to the room.

The Pasha stroked his chin, as if he were teasing out a
difficult problem in his mind. The Pashanne continued
to gaze at Bartlett and Jacques closely. The Conductor of
Ceremonies waited patiently. He was accustomed to
standing around through long, tedious events, and
even enjoyed it. In fact, it was not at all clear that the
Conductor of Ceremonies needed to be there, since there
was actually no ceremony taking place, and therefore
there was nothing to conduct. It was more of a meeting.
But it *was* happening in the throne room, and in the
Conductor's opinion that was enough to make it a
ceremony in *principle*, even if it wasn't a ceremony in
practice. Once he started talking like that, no one could
be bothered arguing with him. He was tall, thin and
straight, and wore a uniform that he had invented himself, consisting of sky blue breeches and an olive green
jacket that came down to his knees, with two breast
pockets and a collar that fitted tightly at the neck. He
also wore a long wig of curly brown hair, which, he
thought, added to the dignity of his Conductions.

Still no one spoke. Bartlett was beginning to wonder

if anyone ever said *anything* in this place. He and Jacques had already been standing there for ten minutes. And it was two *days* since they had arrived in the city. As soon as the Pasha had awoken from his faint, he had them taken away by the guards and locked in a room in the palace. The room was small but bright, the furniture simple but comfortable, their meals plain but filling, the fresh clothes they had been given coarse but clean. Their food had been brought and laid silently on their table by a guard who never uttered a word. It was as if they were not quite prisoners, not quite guests. It was about time they found out just *what* they were.

And Bartlett wanted to know something else. Where was Gozo?

Bartlett looked around to see whether Gozo was there. His own face stared at him from the big mirror on the back wall. When he looked at the Pasha again, the Pasha was still stroking his chin, stroking and stroking.

It was getting ridiculous. If someone didn't speak soon, they might as well go back to their room and wait for dinner.

'Pasha, I have a question.'

'Yes,' said the Pasha, who didn't seem at all surprised to hear Bartlett speak up. 'So do I. I can't decide whether to thank you or hang you. On the one hand,' the Pasha murmured, 'you brought him back. But on the other hand, you probably kidnapped him in the first place.

Then again, you didn't harm him. But on the other hand, you should never have had him at all.'

'Pasha, what have you done with our friend?'

'You've changed him, that's for sure,' said the Pasha. 'He talks all kinds of nonsense . . .'

'You see, I'm responsible for him,' said Bartlett, 'because he isn't a real explorer . . .'

'He was much quieter before he was taken . . .'

'He just joined us, to see what it was like to be an explorer . . .'

'And now Darian seems to be . . .'

'But Gozo has always been . . .'

'Quite excitable.'

'Quite excitable.'

The Pasha frowned. 'Gozo?'

'Darian?' said Bartlett.

They stared at each other. The Pashanne spoke. 'Who is Gozo?'

'Gozo is the boy who came with us, and as soon as we can have him back, we'll be ready to leave.'

'Have him back?' said the Pasha. 'Have him *back*?'

The Pashanne's sharp eyes continued to gaze at Bartlett. 'Why do you call him Gozo?'

'That'll just be the name they gave him, dear,' whispered the Pasha, as if he were a great expert on the matter. 'They use all kinds of names in the Underground.'

'Why?' repeated the Pashanne, speaking to Bartlett.

'It's his name.'

'Who gave it to him? Did you?'

Bartlett laughed. 'Not me. His parents, I suppose.'

'His parents?' boomed the Pasha, rising from his throne. Suddenly his anger got the better of him. His eyes bulged and his face was red. This wasn't something that pomegranates and honeycomb could make up for! '*Gozo*? A name like that? Guards, hang them! I've decided. *Hang them!*'

'*Hang them!* . . . *Hang them!* . . . *Hang them!* . . .' echoed the Pasha's voice in the huge, empty throne room.

'No,' said the Pashanne sharply.

The guards hesitated.

'Wait. Just a moment,' mumbled the Pasha, glancing at his wife and sitting down again.

'Did you kidnap him?' said the Pashanne.

'Of course not,' said Bartlett, 'he wanted to come.'

'He wanted to come!' cried the Pasha, and he started to jump up again, but the Pashanne stopped him with a quick touch of her hand.

'How do you know?' said the Pashanne.

'He said so.'

'So you took him to the Underground?'

The Underground? What was this *Underground* they kept talking about? 'To the Caverns, the Margoulis Caverns.'

'And yet you brought him out?' said the Pashanne.

'How long did you expect us to stay there?' said Jacques le Grand, who was getting sick of these ridiculous questions.

The Pasha was getting sick of them as well. 'All right. I've decided. I'm going to hang them. It's final. I'm definitely going to hang them. Guards!'

The Pashanne merely raised an eyebrow, and the guards hesitated again. They often had to hesitate when the Pasha gave an order, to find out whether the Pashanne agreed. She leaned over and whispered in the Pasha's ear: 'If they brought Darian back, they can bring others as well.'

The Pasha stroked his chin. 'And in return we allow them to live?'

'It will be very hard for them to do it if they're dead.'

'True,' said the Pasha. 'All right,' he announced suddenly. 'You, Bartlett, and you, whatever your name is—someone's told me but I've forgotten, so whatever it is . . .'

'Jacques le Grand, dear,' said the Pashanne.

'That's it. Well, I will spare you both, on condition that you return to the Underground and bring more of our people back.'

Bring people back from the Underground? This whole conversation was getting more and more confusing. 'Excuse me,' said Bartlett, 'could you just explain what exactly you're talking about—'

'Explanations? I don't think you're in a position to demand explanations!' cried the Pasha, 'and neither are you, Jacques whatever your name is, so don't even bother asking. Now: go and bring more of our people back!'

The Pasha glanced at his wife. She nodded.

'And if we don't?' said Bartlett.

'If you don't? I'll hang you both right now. So make up your minds. Do you promise?'

'We can only try,' said Bartlett.

'None of this "we can only try". Promise! Yes or no?'

'Otherwise, you hang us?' said Bartlett, just to be clear.

The Pasha nodded.

'I promise.'

'And you,' said the Pasha, 'whatever your name is.'

'Yes,' murmured Jacques.

'Good,' said the Pasha. He sat back in his chair with a very satisfied look on his face. But soon something began to worry him. The look on his face changed. He leaned close to the Pashanne and whispered in her ear. 'Don't you think, my dear, they might just run off as soon as we let them go? They've promised, but how do we know they'll keep their word? Wouldn't it be easier if we just hanged them now? You know how I like to be sure of things. I hate having to guess what other people will do. If I hang them now, I know *exactly* what they'll be doing.'

'Nothing,' said the Pashanne. 'They won't bring anyone back.'

The Pasha frowned. He began to stroke his chin again, stroke after stroke. 'This is very difficult, very difficult,' he muttered, wishing the Pashanne would say something to make it easier.

Suddenly the Pashanne looked at one of the guards. 'The bag. The one the big one's holding. Bring it here.'

The guard stepped down to Jacques. He held out his hand, pointing at the bag containing the maps of the Margoulis Caverns. Jacques glanced at Bartlett. Bartlett shrugged. They could fight the guards, all six of them, and maybe even win, they could fight the Pasha and the Pashanne, they could fight the strange thin man with the jacket that buttoned right up at the throat—but they couldn't fight all the guards in the city. And besides, they still didn't know where Gozo was.

The guard tugged at the bag. Jacques let it go. The guard took it to the Pashanne.

'What's in it?' asked the Pasha.

The Pashanne shrugged. She didn't even open it. She merely dangled the bag in the air, gazing at Bartlett and smiling knowingly. 'Whatever's inside, my guess is they'll be back for it.'

The Pasha frowned. How did she know? Sometimes the Pashanne had the most extraordinary ideas. And yet

38

she was almost always right, *that* was the most extraordinary thing about her.

'Well then,' said the Pasha after a moment, turning back to Bartlett, 'what are you waiting for? Go! Go back to the Underground and get someone.'

'It will take us a day or two to get ready,' said Bartlett. 'We'll need food, and water, and . . . other stuff.'

'Of course. Of course you will. Get what you need and go tomorrow.'

'And you'll have to make sure people don't try to harm us while we're here. They didn't look very friendly when we arrived.'

'Why should they be friendly?' cried the Pasha. 'After all you've done, after all the people you've—'

'Yes,' said the Pashanne, 'we'll make sure. No one will harm you in the City of Sun. You have our promise.' She turned to one of the guards, and with the slightest nod of her head, instructed him what to do. He turned and left the throne room.

'There's another thing we need to know,' said Bartlett, gazing at the Pashanne. 'You see, Goz—I mean, Darian never told us. Who *are* his parents?'

The Pasha's face went red. He jumped again. 'Why? Why do you *need* to know? No, I've changed my mind, I'm definitely going to hang—'

'We,' said the Pashanne. 'We are Darian's parents.'

Chapter 5

Everywhere they went in the city, people gazed at them with fear and hostility. In the bustling streets of the bazaar, across the squares where children played, in the snaking alleys behind the palace, faces turned and watched. Noisy streets fell silent. Crowds divided to let them pass. No one touched them, no one even brushed against them. The Pashanne's instructions had done their job, and Bartlett and Jacques walked as if protected by an invisible barrier. But look behind, at the street through which they had just walked—look up, at the windows and balconies above—look ahead, at the square in front of them—and everywhere there were eyes, watching, waiting, watching.

And everywhere there were whispers, always the same words, always the same tone: 'Pale! Pale as the Moon.'

Yet they could not leave the city, not yet. Gozo was somewhere inside the palace, and there was too much they did not understand. They tried to piece it together. There was something called an Underground, and people were taken there, and the Pasha's son, Darian, had been taken there as well. And now everyone thought that Gozo was Darian, and that they had brought him back. But Gozo wasn't Darian. Why did the Pasha and Pashanne think he was? And why had

41

Darian been taken to the Underground in the first place? And what *was* this Underground, anyway? *Where* was it? How did you get there? Why hadn't the Pasha himself gone to get his son?

They needed to find out. They needed answers to these questions, and others as well. But who would help them?

They found More in an inn near the city gate. He was sitting by himself at a table in the corner, staring unhappily at a cup of wine. He stared and stared, deep in thought. He didn't notice the gasp of astonishment from the other customers as Bartlett and Jacques came in, didn't notice the silence, the way everyone slipped out the door, didn't notice anything, in fact, until Bartlett had sat down on one side of him and Jacques le Grand was on the other, and so there was nowhere he could go, even if he had wanted to escape.

'More,' said Bartlett, 'we've been looking everywhere for you.'

More looked up with a fright. Then he smiled bitterly. 'You! You must be the only ones who have.' More shook his head. 'I heard the Pasha let you go. You should hear what Bargus is saying. *He* captured you. *He* took you prisoner. According to Bargus, I had nothing to do with it. He did it all by himself.'

'Did what?'

'Took you pris—' More glanced at Jacques le Grand. 'Well, don't blame me! He's the one who's saying it. I haven't said anything. People believe Bargus, he's the kind who can talk. They'd never believe *me*.'

Bartlett grinned. 'You'd like to say you took us prisoner, wouldn't you?'

'Of course I would,' More admitted. 'I'm a guardsman, Bartlett. That's what I'm meant to do. But I couldn't . . . well, I couldn't pretend.'

'Are they sending you out to the stonefields again?'

'No. Everyone thinks Bargus is such a hero they've said he never has to go back there. And because he's such a good *friend*, he's asked them to say that I don't have to go back as well.'

'At least he did that.'

'Only because I asked him, Bartlett—and because I told him that if he didn't, I'd tell everybody what really happened!'

Bartlett laughed.

'It's not funny, Bartlett! I'm really disappointed. Bargus thinks he's going to get into the palace guard. He's going to see the captain tomorrow. He says the day he captured you was the best day of his life. After he gets into the palace guard, he'll probably never talk to me again.'

More took an angry sip of his wine.

'More,' said Bartlett. 'We need your help.'

'Help? What kind of help?' More looked at Bartlett suspiciously. The innkeeper looked at him suspiciously as well. He had crept out from his wine room to see what the two strangers were doing. They were bad for business. All his customers had disappeared, and every time anyone put their head round the doorway they retreated as soon as they saw who was sitting in the corner.

'You can start by telling us what the Underground is,' said Bartlett.

'Me tell *you*?' said More. 'You *know* what the Underground is—that's where you come from!'

Bartlett shook his head.

'But look at yourselves, Bartlett: Pale as the Moon. And how else did you get into the middle of the stonefields? Fly?'

'We were exploring caves. For months and months. We've told you already. That's why we're so pale, months and months in the darkness. And it was from the caves that we came out in the stonefields.'

'Yes, but where did the caves *come* from?' demanded More.

'Hundreds of miles away. From another country.'

More gazed even more suspiciously than before. He looked at the innkeeper. The innkeeper shrugged. He had crept closer and closer, overcome by curiosity.

'Well, the Underground,' said More eventually, 'is a place where people live . . .'

'Underground,' echoed the innkeeper, who could never keep silent for long. He always had opinions about things and couldn't resist helping out with interesting conversations between his customers. 'Would you like some wine?'

Jacques le Grand nodded. They had spent all day walking around the city looking for More, and he could have drunk a whole barrel.

'All right. Don't say anything until I get back,' said the innkeeper, in case he was going to miss anything. 'My name's Sol, by the way.'

'And we're Bartlett and—'

'Jacques le Grand. Everyone knows already.'

'Sol knows everything that goes on in the city,' said More, as the innkeeper went to get the wine. 'He can even tell you the price of spice before the market opens.'

'Twenty cents per grimble,' cried Sol over his shoulder, 'don't pay a cent more.' He disappeared and came back with a wine jug and cups. 'Now,' he said, pulling up a chair and pouring wine for everybody, 'you were asking about the Underground? It's full of people who never come into the sun. They live *under* the ground, instead of on top of it like everyone else.'

'Like you,' added More.

'More, for the last time, we are *not* from the Underground. We love the sun. We live on top of the earth and only go under it when we have to explore.'

'All right,' muttered More.

'So, you're explorers!' cried Sol. 'I knew it. I knew it

as soon as you walked in. Explorers, I said to myself. Where have you been? What have you done? Tell me everything. Have you climbed to the top of the tallest alps? Have you swum to the bottom of the salty sea?'

'The Underground,' said Bartlett. 'Tell us about it. Where is it?'

'In the stonefields,' said More.

'Where in the stonefields?'

More was silent. Bartlett turned to the innkeeper.

Sol shrugged. 'No one knows. That's why the guards go there, to find the Underground, to capture its people if they come out.'

'To capture its people?'

'The people from the Underground,' said Sol suddenly, keeping his voice low and his eyes narrowed, 'are our enemies. They have always been our enemies. They envy us. Here in the City of Sun, we have light, we have brightness. What do they have? Darkness and gloom. They cannot have the sun, so they take *us* instead. They kidnap us whenever they can.'

'Why would they kidnap you? What would do they do—'

'Envy, envy! Listen, centuries ago they arrived. Where did they come from? Out of the ground! What did they want? To invade us, to take our land, to drive us away. But *we* drove them back instead. They learned their lesson! They've stayed where they belong. But they can't forget how we defeated them, they can't forgive us for having all the things that they do not. So they kidnap

46

our people, out of envy and spite. Who knows what they make them do down there in the darkness? Who can imagine what it's like in that place?' Sol shivered with loathing. 'Our people are slaves, prisoners. Many have been taken.'

'How many?'

'Many.'

'Who?'

Sol frowned, thinking. 'There was a goatherd once. I heard about it from his brother. It was his brother who told us, wasn't it, More?'

'I thought it was his uncle.'

'His uncle? No, it was his brother . . .'

Sol scratched his head, trying to remember.

'It doesn't matter,' said Bartlett.

'Of course it matters!' said Sol. 'If you can't tell your brother from your uncle, life can be very difficult.'

'Just one?' said Bartlett. 'Just one goatherd?'

Sol waved an arm. 'Many have been taken, Bartlett.

Why do you question? Now listen. The one they want most is the Pasha. But because they couldn't get him, they took his son instead. They waited. They planned.'

Sol took a deep draught of his wine.

'It was over a year ago. The boy was out hunting with some other princes. It was his first journey out of the city. Many long hours the Pasha and Pashanne thought about it, discussed it, considered it. Would he be safe? Should they let him go? But the boy was insistent, and the other princes said they would look after him well, and the guards swore that they would let nothing happen—and in the end, they agreed. After all, they couldn't keep the boy within the city forever. He was no longer a child, he was growing up. So he went. They hunted all day. They rode far. When night fell they decided to sleep at a well. Others had slept there before. There were at least thirty of them with him. What could happen? In the morning, when the others woke up, he was gone.'

The innkeeper snapped his fingers, as if he were a magician casting a spell.

Bartlett looked at More. 'Is this true?'

More nodded.

Jacques shook his head slightly, so small a movement that no one but Bartlett would have noticed. People can walk off. People can get up in the night and go for a stroll, fall into a ditch and break a leg, get caught by a wild animal, get knocked on the head by a falling rock, get struck by lightning . . . There are hundreds of reasons someone doesn't come back. It didn't mean someone had kidnapped him.

'He was never found,' said the innkeeper in a low voice, leaning forward over his wine cup. 'Not to this day. Not a trace. Not a footstep . . . Not a hair. Do you wonder that we hate them so much? Do you wonder that we send our brave guards to the Stonefields to capture them?'

'What do they look like?' Bartlett asked.

'Pale as the Moon.'

'And?'

'Go on, More,' said Sol. 'You're a guard. You must have seen hundreds of them.'

'Well . . . pale . . .'

'And?'

More bit his lip. 'I've never actually seen one, Bartlett.'

'What about Bargus? He must have seen one.'

More shook his head.

'More!' cried Sol. 'What do you do out there, month after month? You're meant to be a brave guard keeping us safe. Never seen one? Never seen even *one*?'

'There aren't that many around.'

The innkeeper took a mouthful of wine and swallowed it angrily.

'Do you know *anyone* who's seen one?' asked Bartlett.

More shook his head again. 'You don't understand. They're hard to catch. And besides,' he said, raising a fist, 'the guards keep them away. They don't dare show their heads when we're around.'

'Oh, please!' said Sol. 'Never seen even one! More, I'm disappointed. I expected more.'

'Very funny.'

'And you say they're in the stonefields, these people, this . . . Underground?' said Bartlett. 'But you don't know where.'

More nodded.

'Don't blame him,' said Sol, as if he suddenly decided More needed a defender after he had finished attacking him himself. 'No one knows where. If we did, that would be the end of our problems—we'd get rid of them ourselves! But now it's up to you. You have to go back and get the others.' He raised his cup. 'Here's to you, Bartlett and Jacques le Grand. Good luck, go swiftly, return safely—or the Pasha will hang you.'

Sol and More drank to the mission. Yes, thought Bartlett, it was all *much* clearer now. All they had to do, apparently, was outsmart a gang of kidnappers that no one had ever seen in a place that no one could find. He glanced at Jacques, who shrugged. They grinned, tossed back their heads and drained their cups as well.

'There's just one other thing we need you to help us with, More,' said Bartlett, when all the cups had been placed on the table again. 'There's someone we need to see before we leave.'

Chapter 6

The next day Bartlett and Jacques le Grand waited for More at the inn. Sol couldn't let them sit downstairs because they frightened all the customers away. So they waited in a small room on top of the stables, staring at a picture of a sandstorm that hung on the wall.

The day was hot. The hours passed slowly. Jacques lay on a bed. Bartlett sat on a chair. Jacques gazed at the picture. Bartlett's gaze shifted restlessly around the room.

'Jacques.'

Jacques looked at him silently. He was one of those people who rarely speak, but for every word that passed his lips he thought ten times as many thoughts as any other person. He and Bartlett had been friends for so long that when Jacques wanted to say something to him, a glance was usually enough. It was Bartlett who did the talking.

'Jacques, I *know* it's not a real promise. The Pasha threatened to hang us. Promises under threats don't count.'

Jacques nodded.

'But we should keep it.'

Jacques raised an eyebrow.

'Jacques, explorers keep their promises. We both know that. "If you can't trust an explorer's word, you can't trust the sun to rise or the rain to fall." Do you know who used to say that? Sutton Pufrock. He taught me everything I know.'

Jacques knew. He knew about Sutton Pufrock, who had been the greatest explorer of his day. He was old now, of course, and rarely got out of bed, yet that didn't stop him telling everyone else what explorers should do. But Jacques was just as honest as Sutton Pufrock had ever been, he was as trustworthy an explorer as had ever crossed a desert or swum a river. And Jacques knew that promises under threats don't count. Not even Sutton Pufrock would say they did.

'Jacques, I've never failed to keep a promise yet, and neither have you. I *want* to keep it.'

Jacques didn't reply.

'All right. We made the promise because the Pasha was going to hang us. But the maps? What about them? Are we just going to leave them behind?'

Jacques' gaze hardened. The maps! All those months of effort, those terrible dark days under the earth. It was the maps that showed where they had been.

'And Gozo? What about Gozo? What are we going to do, leave him here forever?'

Jacques grinned. Where was Gozo, anyway? In the palace. He was probably being treated like a prince. After all, everyone thought he *was* a prince. It must be better then driving wagons full of melidrops. He probably *did* want to stay forever.

'Jacques, I promised to look after him. Remember? All right, so he's enjoying himself. He's living like a prince, eating sweets and drinking honey and sleeping in a great big bed with seven cushions. So? What happens if Darian comes back? What then? They'll say he's a pretender and chop off his head.'

Jacques wasn't convinced. Why should Darian come back? Where was he meant to come back *from*? Surely Bartlett didn't believe all this nonsense about kidnappers from the Underground! It was the kind of story you tell little children when they're naughty. Only here, *everyone* seemed to believe it. No, people disappeared sometimes. It happened everywhere. You didn't need kidnappers to explain it.

'I don't know, Jacques. I don't know whether I believe it or not. It does sound ridiculous, doesn't it? People who live underground and go kidnapping for their Sunday entertainment. But those stonefields, Jacques, have you ever seen anything like them? Who knows what kind of people live there?' Bartlett got up and began to pace around the room. It wasn't a very big room and it didn't take many paces before he had got around it. He folded his arms and looked at Jacques. 'We'd better hope these people *do* exist,' he said. 'We'd better hope they *do* have the Pasha's son.

Because I've got a feeling the only way we're going to get the maps is to bring someone back. And if we're going to get Gozo—it will have to be Darian.' Bartlett frowned. 'If you ask me, Jacques, it's not going to be easy. It's going to take all the tools of an explorer to do it: Inventiveness, Desperation and Perseverance.'

Bartlett paced again, then he stopped. For a moment the frown stayed on his face, then it disappeared. The beginnings of a smile replaced it. It was that old, familiar sensation, and Jacques felt it as well. As strong as an onion, as sweet as a melidrop, enough to make the hairs of your neck stand up and the skin of your knuckles tingle with excitement: the feeling of an adventure that was about to begin.

Chapter 1

The sun had already set when More came back. He led them swiftly along narrow, twisting alleys. When someone came towards them they pressed themselves into shadows along walls. When an open window glowed with light and hummed with voices they crouched and slipped deftly under it. They passed through the alleys of the city like moonlight gliding over rock.

Finally More stopped in a lane. A wall towered above them. From a window, high up, a shaft of light poked out into the darkness. They were at the back of the palace.

'Here.'

Bartlett looked up at the window. 'You're sure?'

More nodded. He whispered. 'See? I told you, it's no use. I haven't got a ladder. I couldn't find one long enough. I'm sorry, I haven't been much help.'

'Don't be sorry.' Bartlett was looking at the wall. Jacques had been examining it. It was made of the white stone of the city, but since it was the back wall of the palace, the masons had taken little time over it. The stones had been roughly cut, set in place unpolished. There were crevices and cracks, bumps and corners. Jacques was running his hand over them. Now he gripped at the edges of a stone, testing it with his fingers.

Jacques nodded. Bartlett grinned. For someone who had climbed cliffs in the Alps with his fingertips, this was a picnic. And before More could even cry out in surprise, they were both scurrying up the wall like spiders, gripping the sharp corners of the stones with their fingers and pushing themselves up with their feet.

The window was covered with a thick metal grille. Bartlett and Jacques held on to it as they looked inside. The light was coming from a bright lantern hanging

in the middle of the room. Directly beneath it was a fountain: water rose out of the trunk of a little carved elephant, no bigger than a pineapple, and splashed into a pool. There was a big bed with orange curtains, and a divan with orange cushions, and a table with golden dishes and a big golden jug. And lying on the divan, munching a sweet, was Gozo.

'*Gozo!*'

Gozo looked around. He frowned, wondering whether he had heard anything, and then he decided that he hadn't, and his frown disappeared, and his hand reached out towards the golden dishes on the table again.

'Gozo! Over here, at the window!'

Now Gozo jumped up. He ran to the window. 'Mr Bartlett,' he cried excitedly. 'What are you doing out there? That's a very difficult way to arrive! I don't think—'

'Gozo, quiet! We're not meant to be here.'

Gozo's eyes went wide. 'Not meant to be here?' He noticed Jacques le Grand. 'Hello, Jacques,' he said. 'Are you not meant to be here as well?'

Jacques shook his head.

Gozo looked puzzled. 'I've been waiting for you to come, you know.'

Bartlett nodded. 'Are you all right?'

'Oh, yes, Mr Bartlett!' cried Gozo, forgetting he was meant to keep his voice down. 'It's wonderful. I've never had so much cream and marzipan.'

'And honey?'

'Yes, honey as well.'

'And oranges?'

'Some oranges. I don't like oranges so much, you know. And pomegranates, Mr Bartlett. The Pasha's always giving me pomegranates, but I don't like them one bit. They're all seeds! I've told him to get himself a dozen fresh melidrops, but he doesn't know what they are. He doesn't even believe they exist. Of course, I said we could get him some, but when I started to tell him we'd need to go on an ice voyage first, he didn't believe that either! And there are other strange things about the people here as well. For instance, they call me a strange name—'

'Darian?'

Gozo stared. 'How did you know?'

'Gozo,' said Bartlett, 'do you know who they think you are?'

'Who they *think* I am?' Gozo frowned. 'Well, I just thought they didn't like the name Gozo, so they decided to use another one.'

'The Pasha's son!'

'The Pasha's son!' Gozo yelped excitedly.

'Gozo, quiet!'

'Well, that explains a lot,' whispered Gozo. 'The Pashanne keeps hugging me. She even tries to kiss me! I told her to stop it.'

'And they want to keep you here forever.'

'Forever!' Gozo yelped again. 'Well, it *is* very nice here . . . and I've never had so much cream . . .'

'And marzipan,' added Jacques, in case Gozo had forgotten.

'But I don't think . . . forever . . . that's a long time, Mr Bartlett, that's . . . that's . . .'

'Forever.'

'Exactly. No, I don't think I'd like that. I'd never see anyone again, my family, or the farm, or you, Mr Bartlett, or you, Jacques. No, that won't do at all.'

'Good,' said Bartlett. 'Because what we've got to do is—'

'Gozo!'

It was a woman's voice. Bartlett froze. So did Gozo and Jacques.

'Who's that?' whispered Bartlett.

'Gozo, what are you doing at the window?'

'You'd better go, Mr Bartlett, before she sees you.'

But Bartlett stayed. The other person who had just

come into the room had said *Gozo*. Not Darian. This woman, whoever she was, knew that Gozo wasn't the Pasha's son!

'*Gozo?*'

The voice was closer. Now Bartlett could see her. She was a small, bent woman, and a big bunch of keys hung from her belt.

'Hello,' said Bartlett loudly.

The woman approached the window suspiciously. 'Who's there?'

'Bartlett.'

'Bartlett?'

'And Jacques le Grand.'

Now the woman had come right up to the window. She poked her nose against the bars. 'What's holding you up out there?'

'Nothing,' said Bartlett.

The woman ran her
fingers over one of
Bartlett's hands, as
if to make sure she
wasn't imagining
things. 'Well, you
are a very brave boy,'
she said, 'and so are
you,' she added,
glancing at Jacques.

'Thank you, Madam,'
said Bartlett. 'Actually, my arms

are starting to ache so I won't stay long.'

'No, don't wear yourself out.'

'We just wanted to see Gozo. We're the ones who brought him.'

'Oh, well, in that case, of course you want to see him. You must be missing him.'

'Yes,' said Bartlett. 'We'd like him back, actually, wouldn't we Jacques. *Jacques?*'

'Yes, I wish I could give him to you,' said the woman.

'Don't you like him?'

'Of course I like him.' She put an arm around Gozo's shoulder. She was so small and hunched that she had to reach up to do it. 'How couldn't I like him? But . . .'

'But what?'

The old woman didn't say.

'He isn't Darian, is he?' said Bartlett.

The woman shook her head. 'No, Bartlett, he isn't. He looks like Darian, it's almost frightening, how close they are. But, you see, I was Darian's nurse. My name is Mirta and I was with him every day. Every day except for that . . . that terrible day when they took him out hunting. He wasn't ready to go, Bartlett. He was still too young.' For a moment Mirta's eyes filled with tears. 'He grew up in front of my eyes. I could *never* mistake him for another.'

'Can't you tell the Pasha that Gozo isn't his son?'

'I've tried. But the Pasha and the Pashanne *want* to believe it's him. You see, they miss Darian so much, and now they've convinced themselves he's come back.

Nothing will convince them otherwise. Not even all the stories he tells, like travelling to the freezing seas. What an imagination he has!'

'Mr Bartlett, tell her it's true!'

'We only want to take him home, Mirta.'

'I know, he should go home.' She shrugged helplessly.

'And we will take him. Do you know how? We're going to bring Darian back!'

Mirta shook her head sadly. 'No one can bring Darian back, Bartlett.'

'If anyone can, it's us!'

Mirta didn't reply. She gazed at Bartlett, perhaps trying not to have too much hope.

'It's true,' said Bartlett. 'Listen, Gozo: we'll be back. And whatever happens, don't be discouraged. Perseverance, remember? Whatever anyone says, we'll be back. And when we arrive, we'll bring the most amazing thing you've seen in your life: someone who looks just like you.'

'Exactly the same?' cried Gozo excitedly.

'Well, almost,' said Bartlett, glancing at Mirta.

Mirta smiled, but there was much sadness in her eyes. 'Good luck,' she whispered, as Bartlett and Jacques le Grand disappeared like two dark spiders down the side of the wall.

Chapter 8

Back to the stonefields marched Bartlett and Jacques le Grand. Back along the road, where people came out to look at them from their tents, back through the grasses, where the goatherds gazed up from their distant flocks, back across the sands, where their feet left a long, twisting trail behind them. And then . . . the red rock stretched ahead of them once more. Its vast boulders dotted the landscape. Its jagged pillars rose against the horizon. It neither welcomed nor rejected them, but was merely *there*, as it had always been there, yesterday and tomorrow, without beginning or end, and two people, two human beings more or two human beings less upon it, was not a matter of the slightest concern.

Bartlett and Jacques paused before it. The emptiness seemed to stretch forever. It was the moment that every explorer knows, that last moment before he or she sets foot into the desert, climbs the first cliff of the mountain, pushes off from the river bank—the instant when suddenly there is nothing ahead but the unknown. It is a moment of fear, of uncertainty and doubt, and no explorer can avoid it, no matter how experienced or brave. Faced with it for the first time, some turn back and never try again. But the true explorer, trusting to Inventiveness, Desperation and Perseverance, steps forward.

'By the way, Jacques,' murmured Bartlett, still staring

at the rock, 'I don't suppose you have any idea how to find the Underground?'

Jacques shook his head.

'No,' said Bartlett, 'neither have I.'

And they looked at each other, grinned, and together, without another word, at exactly the same instant, stepped forward onto the rust-red rock that lay ahead.

They marched deep into the stonefields. For day after day they passed through valleys and over hills of rock. They saw no one else. In the day the sun beat down as in the hottest of deserts, and at night the air turned to frost and the moon rose pale and cold into the sky. They walked amongst the pillars of stone, they wandered amongst the looming boulders, they searched, but what were they searching for? Into each opening in the rock, each cave, they peered, listened, cried out, but there was no answer but the echo of their own voices. Where was the Underground? How did it begin? As a crevice? As a hole? And if the opening was covered by stone, how would they recognise it? There was rock everywhere. Any boulder might cover the entrance. They crouched amongst the pebbles at the base of great lumps of rock, looking for signs that they had been moved. But how many boulders were there in the stonefields? Hundreds? Thousands? It would take years to check them all.

They came upon the valley where they had first entered the stonefields. There, on the hillside, was the opening of the Margoulis Caverns, and there, in the distance, was the clump of boulders where Bargus and More had 'captured' them. Perhaps the Underground was in the Margoulis Caverns. Perhaps it led off the main caves into a part that they had not discovered. But they had mapped every inch, explored every passage, crawled into every tunnel until it came to an end or grew too small for a human being to follow. No, they wouldn't find the Underground there. It was elsewhere—*if* it existed.

That was the question that played on their minds, never going away, no matter how much they tried to get rid of it. From the very beginning Jacques had doubted that there was such a thing as the Underground, that there had ever been such a thing, that it was anything more than the name people give to their own fears. It was this doubt that Bartlett tried to squash. Perseverance, he said to himself, just as Sutton Pufrock would have said it, Perseverance, he repeated, as his feet marched over the red rock, one after the other, right after left, left after right, right, left, right, left, Perseverance, Perseverance, Perseverance, Perseverance . . .

Jacques stopped and gave him a curious glance.

'Well, what else can we do Jacques? How else are we going to get Gozo back? Or the maps?'

'You don't have to sing about it,' Jacques muttered.

'I wasn't singing!' Bartlett paused. 'Was I singing? I wasn't singing "Perseverance", was I?'

Jacques grinned.

'Well, why not?' said Bartlett. 'It's a very good word. It's a very good song for an explorer. In fact, I can't think of a better one. Perseverance!' he cried, and after a second the rocks sent back their echo: *'Perseverance!'*

Jacques shook his head, and began walking again. Bartlett quickly caught up with him, chanting 'Perseverance, Perseverance,' until Jacques put his hands over his ears and began to run.

Yet Perseverance alone did not ensure success. The days passed. Sol had given them food but now it was running low. They would have to leave the stonefields. Yet they had found nothing. They had searched in vain.

That night, after they had eaten a tiny portion of the dry biscuits that remained, Jacques gazed questioningly at Bartlett. He didn't need to speak. What would they do? They had found no sign of the Underground, no trace of its people. And without this, without *something*, Gozo and the maps of the Margoulis Caverns would remain locked within the Pasha's palace, far from their grasp, forever.

The next morning they awoke early. It was as if, knowing that they had little time left to search in the stonefields, they could not allow themselves to sleep longer. The eastern sky was barely beginning to lighten. They climbed the hill beneath which they had slept. In the valley below, as the sun rose, two guards lay asleep in their cloaks.

Chapter 9

Bartlett and Jacques ran down the hill. They grabbed the guards' spears as they slept.

Bartlett prodded them. 'Wake up. You're our prisoners.'

'We're from the Underground,' added Jacques, who couldn't resist.

The guardsmen stared at them with fright and horror. It was as if they had awoken into their most feared nightmare. Their eyes were wide, their mouths were open, their hair stood on end, and neither of them could utter a sound. Then Bartlett and Jacques sat down beside them, laughing, and told them that they, too, were looking for the Underground.

It took a while for the guardsmen to recover from the shock. One of them was constantly jumping and fidgeting. He wouldn't let go of his spear once he had it in his hand again, wouldn't sit down to eat. His companion, meanwhile, took out their food and began to share it. It wasn't very pleasant, just some dry biscuit, crumbly white cheese and a fig each. Bartlett and Jacques took it gratefully.

'So, you haven't found the Underground yet?' said the guardsman, as he munched some cheese.

'No,' said Bartlett.

'Well, I'm sure it won't be long until you do,' he said mockingly.

'Do you know where we should look?'

The guardsman laughed, shaking his head. A question like that was too ridiculous to even try to answer.

'If you ask me, *they* know.'

It was the other guard who had suddenly spoken. He was still standing, clutching his spear. Bartlett turned to look at him. 'Who knows?'

'They watch, that's why.' He leaned closer, whispering, '*They* see everything. Even now. *They're watching*.' He turned to Jacques. 'They're watching you, too!'

Everyone looked around. There was nothing but rock. Columns of stone stood nearby.

68

'The rocks have eyes,' said the nervous guard, who sounded completely mad. He giggled. Then he looked at his companion. He hunched his shoulders. 'Come on, we've been here too long.'

The other guard glanced at Bartlett and rolled his eyes, indicating what he thought of his friend's ideas. Too many months in the stonefields, too many years, until the columns of rock began to look like people and when you glanced suddenly over your shoulder you could swear that you had seen them move. Even Bartlett had seen, once or twice, imaginary movements of columns and other tricks that his eyes played on him in this vast emptiness of stone.

The other guard gathered up his cloak, put the food away and picked up his spear.

Suddenly the first guard pointed his finger at Bartlett. 'They know you. They *see* you.' And he walked away without another word.

His companion followed him.

Jacques laughed. But Bartlett didn't respond. He was deep in thought, watching the guards disappear over the hill.

That morning, Bartlett and Jacques headed out of the stonefields. Empty and blank, the rocks did not reveal their secret. But Bartlett had stopped searching. He was leaving as quickly as he could, heading for the grasslands where they could get food.

They were given bread and cheese by a goatherd who tended his goats on the dusty plains.

'And now?' said Jacques.

'We're going back,' said Bartlett, slinging his bag over his shoulder.

Jacques watched him silently. What was the point of wandering around the stonefields again? What made Bartlett think they were going to find anything this time? Too much Perseverance was just as dangerous as too little.

'Inventiveness!' said Bartlett, holding up one of his knobbly fingers. A big grin came across his face. 'Not Perseverance by itself—Inventiveness as well. I have an idea. We're not going to wander around again. Don't you see? That's the whole point, Jacques.'

What was the whole point?

'We're not going to wander this time. We're going to sit.'

Chapter 10

They went back to the stonefields, deep into the stone-fields—and they sat. Not on a hill, where they could have seen everything around them, but in a valley, below hills from which they could be seen. Not in the shade of boulders, where they would have been hidden, but in the open, despite the heat of the sun. They sat, and in the night they slept, and in the day they sat again.

Perhaps it was the hardest thing an explorer can do—not to climb cliffs until his arms are ready to fall off, or to push through sand until his legs feel like lead, or to march through a blizzard until his whole body is numb, but to sit, still, for hour after hour, day after day, and wait. Yet that was what they had decided to do.

Why? The idea, in a way, was simple, so simple, that, like many of the most powerful ideas, no one had ever thought of it before. Even Jacques, when Bartlett explained it, had to agree. It was something the crazy guardsman had said. Two words: *They're watching*.

These were the words that had made Bartlett think. The Underground—if there *was* such a place, as Jacques interrupted to remind him—was hidden. That was obvious. But if you lived in such a place, and there were guards looking for you, how could you be sure to remain concealed? And if you ever wanted to come out, even if it was only to kidnap someone, how could you do it without being discovered . . . unless you *already* knew where the guards were? Only then would you know when and where it was safe to emerge. In short, the people from the Underground—if there *were* such people, as Jacques pointed out—must be keeping watch. They must see the guardsmen wandering in pairs across the valleys. They must know where they were, where they walked, where they slept. The crazy guard had to be right—how else could you explain the fact that no one ever found them?

'*If* they exist,' said Jacques again, just to remind Bartlett why all these theories didn't really matter anyway.

Bartlett shrugged. The people from the Underground must have seen *them*, Bartlett and Jacques, wandering as well. And this was where Bartlett's idea started: as long as they wandered, the people from the Underground would feel safe, because that was normal. They saw it every day, they had seen the guards wander for years. One more pair of wanderers wouldn't interest them. But what if he and Jacques *stopped*? What if they simply sat? This would be something new. This would worry them. Why were these two people doing it? Why weren't they walking? What were they planning to do? Day after day, as Bartlett and Jacques sat, the questions would grow, the curiosity would become greater. And eventually, if they waited long enough, someone would come to find out . . .

'Jacques,' said Bartlett, 'there's nothing that worries

people as much as something unexpected—a change in a pattern.'

Jacques nodded. Bartlett was right. He almost forgot to add an '*if* they exist' as he thought about it.

To turn things back to front—to make the wanderers watch, and the watchers wander, that was Bartlett's plan.

They sat for four days. On the fourth night, the pale moon rose over the stonefields as they slept. The dew lay cold on the rocks as the fifth day dawned.

Bartlett was just waking up. His eyes had opened. He saw a movement. What was it? A pillar of stone that stood nearby. He blinked. No, he must still be asleep. It must be his imagination—like the other imaginary movements of columns that he had seen before, and the other tricks your eyes played on you in this emptiness of stone.

But he wasn't asleep. And it wasn't his imagination.
The pillar moved. It *moved*. Bartlett
sat up. The pillar was turning on
itself, swivelling. And suddenly
there was an arm, and then a leg,
and then . . . a person was
standing in front of
them.

He wasn't very tall.
His face was pale, and he had a small
moustache, which wasn't very thick,
because he was quite young. He wore
a round goat's-hair hat on
his head.

He had brown eyes, and they were
staring intently at Bartlett.

'Jacques,' said Bartlett, reaching out to

 shake Jacques' shoulder, as Jacques continued to snore peacefully. Bartlett had not shifted his gaze from the young stranger's face. 'Jacques, I think you'd better wake up.'

Chapter 11

Suddenly the young man began talking very quickly and nervously.

'Who are you? What are you doing here? Why don't you go?'

Bartlett started to stand up.

'Don't move! Do as I say! I'm not alone!'

Bartlett looked around. 'You look like you're alone.'

'I'm not!'

'All right,' said Bartlett. He stood up slowly. 'I'm a bit stiff, you see, from all the sitting I've been doing. I'm Bartlett, and this is Jacques le Grand.'

Jacques was awake now, and gazing at the stranger with curiosity.

'This fellow came out from that pillar over there,' Bartlett explained to Jacques. He turned to look back at the stranger. 'What's your name?'

'I asked you first.'

'I've told you already. Now, who are *you*?'

'I don't have to tell you. Go! Why don't you go? What are you doing here?'

Bartlett waited. He kept his eye steadily on the young man's face. After a moment the young man dropped his gaze.

'Avner.'

'Avner,' Bartlett repeated, stepping forward with his

hand outstretched.

Avner shook his hand reluctantly. He shook Jacques' hand as well.

'You realise that if you refuse to go I'll have to take you prisoner?' Avner said suddenly.

'Of course,' said Bartlett. 'You kidnap people all the time, don't you?'

Avner waited. 'Well? Aren't you going to run away? Look, I haven't even got a knife. I haven't even got a stick to hit you with.'

Bartlett shrugged. He glanced at Jacques le Grand. 'You've captured us, Avner. Now you'd better take us with you.'

Whether there were any others watching that day, Bartlett never discovered. Avner led them over a hill and into another valley. Gradually he became more and more talkative.

'We've been wondering what we should do with you. Just sitting there. What's the point? No one just sits there like that. It isn't pleasant. It isn't comfortable.'

Jacques le Grand agreed. It wasn't comfortable at all.

'How long have you been wondering?' asked Bartlett.

'How long have you been there?'

'Four days.'

'We've probably been wondering for three and a half. Of course, when you were here before, it was all quite obvious, walking around like all the others. But this time, when you came back, you behaved very strangely, just sitting there.' Avner stopped for a moment. 'You're not . . . you know . . . *mad*, are you?'

'I don't think so,' said Bartlett.

'Because it is quite mad to do that, you know. I hope you don't think I'm insulting you. But it is, really.'

Jacques grinned.

'Of course,' Avner was saying, 'some of us just wanted to keep watch. "No need to talk to them," they said. But how were we going to find out what you were up to? No, someone had to do it. That's why they chose me.'

'Why?'

'Because I'm always talking,' said Avner, which certainly seemed to be true. But then he stopped. They couldn't have been walking for more than half an hour. They were standing in front of a huge pillar. It would have taken four people to put their arms all the way around it.

Avner put his hand on the rock. As quick as a flash, before Bartlett could see how Avner had done it, the pillar swivelled on its base. In an instant it was still again, as if it had never moved. But where it had originally stood there was now a vast gaping hole.

A set of steps descended into the shadows, carved into the red rock.

Bartlett stared in amazement. 'You mean we were this close?'

'You're always close wherever you are on the stone-fields. This is just the entrance we use for new arrivals.'

Jacques shook his head in amazement. Well, the Underground existed, there was no doubt of that.

'And you just brought us here?' said Bartlett. 'Just like that? No blindfold, nothing to stop us finding our way back again?'

Avner was silent.

'What?' said Bartlett.

'No one who comes to this entrance ever has to find his way back again, Bartlett. No one ever leaves.'

Chapter 12

Flames!

At the bottom of the steps, two lines of flames stretched into the darkness.

Avner touched something on the wall, there was a quick creaking noise, and the opening of the steps was covered. The sunlight was gone. The darkness was deeper, the flames were clearer. They flickered, yellow. They were coming from lamps on the walls, and far away they seemed no larger than tiny trembling pin-pricks of light. They marked out a passage that stretched into the darkness ahead of them.

'Come on,' said Avner.

The only light came from the flames. The rock glared red around them, and everywhere else there was shadow. Avner led them along the passage. There were openings into other tunnels which were lit by lamps as well. People began to appear in the openings, to watch them pass. They wore goatskin clothes, like Avner. Some were in shadow, others stood beside lamps and their faces were clearly lit. There was not the hostility in their eyes that Bartlett and Jacques had seen in the City of Sun. There was curiosity, and interest, and Bartlett was sure they would have run forward if Avner had not been shouting: 'No one to talk to them! No one to talk to them! They're going to Prule!'

'What's Prule?' asked Bartlett.

'You'll see,' said Avner, and he shouted again as they passed another curious group of spectators.

Then they turned off the main passage and into a smaller tunnel. After a while it began to twist, and then they turned into another passage, and then into another again. And everywhere it was the same, everything was carved out of rock and lit by the shimmering yellow flames of the lamps.

The passage ended at a door. Avner knocked.

'Is it you?' came a voice.

'Yes,' said Avner.

'Then come in.'

Avner pushed on the door. It squeaked as it opened. He stood back and gestured to Bartlett and Jacques le

81

Grand to enter. Jacques had to duck under the lintel to go in.

They were standing in a large room, lit by three lamps in the corners. It looked like a natural cavern. Its roof bristled with stalactites, its walls were jagged, its floor was uneven. The red rock was mixed with patches of a softer, yellow stone.

The voice had come from a small man who stood in the shadows. He was old, with a long grey beard. His shoulders were not far above his waist. The sleeves on his tunic came down only to his elbows.

'This is Prule,' whispered Avner to Bartlett.

Prule gazed at Bartlett and Jacques in turn, looking into their eyes, as if trying to see inside their thoughts. Then he nodded at Avner. He pulled a stone out of his tunic and turned to the wall. Bartlett heard him scratch the rock twice.

'They call themselves Bartlett and Jacques le Grand,' said Avner.

'Do they?' said Prule. 'That's interesting. Thank you, Avner. Tell the Ahsap I thanked you.'

'I will.'

'Only once, though. Tell him I only thanked you once. Don't exaggerate.'

'I won't, don't worry,' said Avner, and he disappeared, closing the door behind him.

For a moment the old man was silent. Then he began to chuckle. 'The sitters! Everyone knows about you. You're famous.' Prule sat down. A ledge of rock ran around the wall. 'You haven't seen much of our home yet. Eventually you will. It's a wonderful place. There are tunnels and caverns you can hardly begin to imagine. But come and sit. You must be tired.'

'We don't normally sit all the time, Prule,' said Bartlett. Prule chuckled again.

'That was just a way to make someone come out and talk to us.'

'Well, come and sit down anyway. There's no need to

stand. You're going to be here for a long time, so you may as well get used to it.'

Bartlett sat down. Jacques preferred to remain on his feet, leaning with his back against the door and his arms across his chest.

'How long will we be here?' said Bartlett.

'As long as it takes,' said Prule. 'You see, I look after everyone who's brought here, until they're ready to go out with the others.'

'Out?'

'Into our caverns. Sometimes it's quick, sometimes it takes months. Some people don't adapt very easily.' Prule looked at Jacques and called out cheerfully: 'Come on, Jacques, come and sit down. There's no point standing there like that. I know you're not going to do anything silly. I could see it the moment you walked in. If I'd had any doubts, we'd have put you in there.' Prule pointed to a small door in the wall. 'I'm never mistaken.'

'Not yet,' growled Jacques.

Prule hooted with laughter. He threw his head back so suddenly that his long beard flipped all the way over and covered his face.

Jacques sat down.

'That's better,' said Prule, pulling away the wisps of beard that had stuck in his eyebrows.

'Of course, you realise, Prule, that we may not be staying as long as the others.'

'Of course not, Bartlett, it depends how quickly you adapt. Some adapt slowly and some—'

'No, Prule. Here, under the ground. I don't mean this room.'

'Ah. Well, that's different. Once you arrive, you stay forever. Didn't Avner tell you? He was meant to tell you before he captured you, so you could have the choice. No one else ever gets a choice. You ought to be grateful.'

Excellent, thought Jacques. Just a little detail that Avner got out of sequence.

'Of course, some people's forever is longer than others',' continued Prule, chuckling once more, 'but that's not up to us, is it?'

Bartlett grinned. There was something very welcoming about Prule. He obviously enjoyed his job.

'I like being with people,' Prule explained.

'And I bet people like you.'

'Most of them do,' said Prule modestly, blushing into his beard.

'Well, the thing is, Prule, that we really may *not* be staying as long as the others.'

Prule shook his head, not understanding.

'Think of it this way: we're not like the others, are we? We came into the stonefields and waited to be captured. How many others have arrived like that?'

'None. That's why we gave you the choice.'

'Exactly,' said Bartlett. He leaned closer. 'You see, Prule, we've come here for a reason.'

'A reason?' whispered Prule, his face lighting up with interest. 'What reason?'

Bartlett put a finger to his lips. 'It's a secret. I can't tell you. There's only one person I can tell—your Pasha.'

'We don't have a Pasha.'

'What do you have?'

'We have an Ahsap.'

'Then he's the one I have to tell.'

Prule stood up. He began to pace the uneven floor, skipping over cracks and jumping up on little mounds. He fingered his long grey beard. Once or twice he turned, and peered at Bartlett, and paced again.

'No one's ever come here with a *reason* before,' said Prule eventually. 'Are you sure you can't tell me what it is?'

Bartlett shook his head.

'What about you, Jacques? No? Well, the problem, Bartlett, is very simple. I hardly see the Ahsap. He only comes here once a year to say hello, and it's very kind of him to do it, because he needn't bother.'

'And when was he—'

'Two weeks ago. So you've got almost a whole year to wait!'

Jacques groaned.

'Yes, I'd groan as well, Jacques,' said Prule, and he did, just to show his sympathy.

But Jacques wasn't looking at Prule. He was gazing at Bartlett. A year? Jacques wasn't waiting a *year*, and he wanted to be sure that Bartlett realised it. Suddenly Bartlett had an idea.

'Tell me, Prule,' said Bartlett, 'is your Ahsap a clever man?'

'Oh, yes, very clever. He can multiply numbers with four digits in his head. I can't do more than three myself.'

'And does he—'

'Although he sometimes writes rather silly poems, and everyone has to pretend they're clever. Although, actually, now that you ask about it, some of them *are* quite clever. There was one about a fish and a weevil which I particularly remember:

Said the weevil to the fish,
If you only had one wish,
And the wish you had would never have another,
Would you wish for mounds of wheat,
Where you'd wriggle, roll and eat,
Or . . .'

Prule frowned.

'Where you'd wriggle, roll and eat,
Or . . . Or . . .

No, I can't remember it. It had something about the weevil's mother . . . or maybe it was his brother . . .' Prule shook his head and his whole beard shivered. 'Perhaps it wasn't really as clever as I thought.'

'Just tell me this, Prule. Does he know we're here?'

Prule narrowed his eyes, thinking. 'Well, Avner is supposed to tell him. And presuming he goes straight there—which I'm not absolutely sure he'll do, because he might stop for lunch on the way—and if he walks as fast as I think he walks—and of course I can't be sure he does, because I've never actually seen him walk, except in and out of this room, which isn't really the same thing—but if he *does* walk as fast as he should walk, for a boy of his age, and if he *does* go straight there, which he should do, because it's the Ahsap himself who's waiting, then he should be arriving . . . just about . . . *now*.'

'Good,' said Bartlett.

Good? Jacques rolled his eyes. What was good?

'If the Ahsap really is as clever as you say,' said Bartlett, 'even if he does write silly poems sometimes, then when he learns we're here, and he hears how we were captured—sitting down and *waiting* for someone to find us—then he'll ask himself: "Why?" And if he can multiply numbers with four digits in his head, I'll bet you he'll want to find out.'

And Bartlett glanced back at Jacques, as if to say that *that* was why they weren't going to have to wait a year.

But Jacques didn't find Bartlett's idea particularly convincing, especially when Prule replied, as cheerfully as ever: 'Oh, I don't want to bet against you, Bartlett. If I won, and you did have to wait a year to meet the Ahsap, you'd be very unhappy. That would take all the pleasure out of winning. And I very easily *could* win. The Ahsap's very clever, but who's to say he'll be interested to know why you wanted to be captured? There's something you should know about the Ahsap: if he decides something doesn't interest him, he forgets about it forever.'

Chapter 13

The Underground was a vast network of tunnels and caverns, all hollowed out of the rock, all lit by the flickering flames of oil lamps. Passages ran from room to room, from cavern to cavern. Steps connected one level with another, galleries ran above plunging depths, bridges crossed gushing underground streams, tunnels stretched out to secret openings under pillars all over the stonefields. And in the very centre of this network, excavated from the heart of the red rock by the Underground's finest carvers, was the counsel chamber of the Ahsap.

Here too, light came from lamps on the walls, but the oil in these lamps was the purest and gave off not a whiff of smoke. The rock on which the flames threw their light was smoothed and polished like the flawless surface of a jewel, and the light shimmered on it as if it were made of glass. A criss-cross of grooves had been carved into the floor, so that it seemed to have been laid with perfect rust-red tiles. In the middle of the room was a pool, shaped like a diamond, with a rim that rose from the floor and curved over gently into the water. The ceiling, high above, curved gently as well, and a series of tiny, delicate lanterns was contained within it, carved into the rock itself, from which additional lamps, twinkling like stars in the sky, threw glints of light into the pool below.

And as for the furniture in the room: the counsellors' two benches, which ran gracefully in two arms around the pool, grew directly out of the floor, beautifully carved with delicate patterns and elegant backs. The Ahsap's throne, standing between them, directly opposite the point of the diamond pool, was a masterpiece of the carvers' art, with wonderful fish sculpted along the arm-rests.

It was on this throne that the Ahsap was sitting. He was a slim man, with a thoughtful face, as if he were a man who was more comfortable with ideas than with action. His clothes were of the finest goat's hair imaginable, and his round goat's-hair hat had a silky lustre. On either side of him, the counsellors' benches were full. Closest to him sat the oldest and wisest, then the younger and less experienced, and finally the newest counsellors, the most recently appointed, who barely dared to open their mouths for the first five years that they sat in the chamber.

On the other side of the pool stood Avner, holding his hat and twisting it nervously as the Ahsap questioned him.

'And you captured them, you say?'

Avner nodded.

'Even though you told them they would stay forever?'

'I . . . told them they would stay forever,' said Avner, who would never have dared to lie to the Ahsap.

'And yet they came?'

Avner winced. Fortunately, the closest counsellor on

the Ahsap's left had leaned across and taken his attention by whispering in his ear.

The Ahsap looked back. 'Are they mad, Avner?'

'I . . . don't think so.'

The counsellor on the Ahsap's right leaned across and whispered.

'Are they stupid, then?'

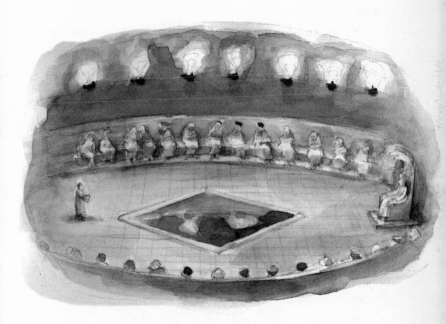

'No,' said Avner. 'They're not stupid at all. But one of them doesn't talk very much.'

'Hmmm,' said the Ahsap. 'Has Prule seen them?'

Avner nodded.

'And? What did he say? Did he tell you to say anything to me?'

'He told me to tell you that he thanked me.'

'How many times?' said the Ahsap sharply.

'Just once. I'm not meant to exaggerate.'

'*Do* you exaggerate, Avner?'

Avner bit his lip. 'Sometimes, Ahsap. But not this time! Prule thanked me once. Honestly he did.'

'Prule is inclined sometimes to be too grateful,' said the Ahsap severely.

'He wasn't *very* grateful, Ahsap. He was just . . . more . . . thankful. And I don't think he was *too* thankful. I wouldn't exaggerate, not in front of you, Ahsap, I mean—*never*, I'd never exaggerate—I mean, never again, because I have, sometimes, you know, I mean, once or twice, but not—I mean—'

'Avner, you're starting to talk like a monkey.'

'Yes, Ahsap.'

'And not a very clever monkey. But you have done a very good job—'

'Oh, thank you, Ahsap!'

'Avner, let me finish. You have done a very good job in bringing these prisoners, and even if Prule is inclined to be too grateful, I am grateful as well—'

'Oh, Ahsap!'

'Avner! I am only a bit grateful. Not as grateful as Prule, that's for sure.' The Ahsap sighed. 'Now I suppose I will have to think about what to do with them.'

'Yes, Ahsap.'

Avner gazed at the Ahsap, still twisting his hat. Nothing happened. The Ahsap seemed to be waiting for him to do something. But what? Avner looked around in confusion. Then he noticed one of the counsellors, cocking his head and moving his eyebrows up and down. And then another one twitched, and another one jerked her head, and soon almost all the counsellors were bobbing and gesturing, and finally Avner realised what they were doing—they were all indicating the door, and trying to tell him that it was time to leave!

'Goodbye, Ahsap.'

'Yes. Goodbye, Avner,' said the Ahsap.

Avner left the room. Everyone watched him silently. He closed the door behind him.

A second later, the counsel chamber exploded with shouts and exclamations.

'Mad!' . . . *'Stupid!'* . . . *'Madness!'* . . . *'Badness!'* . . .

The counsellors were on their feet, shouting and jostling. It was only a matter of time before someone ended up in the pool.

The Ahsap buried his face in his hands. Why did his counsellors always jump and push? Why couldn't they sit and discuss calmly? He was sure *other* people's counsellors did that. And he had had such beautiful benches carved for their use, with lovely soft goat's-hair cushions to make them comfortable. Why could they never *stay* on them?

The Ahsap looked up. The counsellors had calmed down a bit. One or two of them were still hopping around. Now and again someone yelped *'Mad!'* or *'Stupid!'* But it wouldn't last. If he didn't do something soon, they'd be pushing and shoving again as much as before.

'You!' said the Ahsap. 'What do you think?'

'Ahsap!' . . . *'No!'* . . . *'Her?'* cried the counsellors in disbelief. The Ahsap had turned to the very youngest one there. She had been appointed to the counsel only a month before. So young was she, in comparison with all the aged and experienced counsellors in the room, and so new was she, that she barely had the right to jump up and push, much less speak directly to the Ahsap. She, alone of all the counsellors in the chamber, had stayed in her seat.

'Quiet!' demanded the Ahsap.

The counsellors shuffled their feet. They murmured under their breaths. But everyone looked at the counsellor at the very end of the bench, waiting to see what she would do.

'I . . . I don't know if they're mad or stupid—'

'See! . . . *'She doesn't know!'* . . . *'She doesn't—'*

'Quiet! Qui—*et!*'

The counsellor cleared her throat. 'I don't . . . know. But this is what I think—if they're not mad, and they're not stupid—'

'If!' . . . *'If!'* cried the other counsellors contemptuously.

'If they're not mad or stupid,' said the counsellor, gaining confidence as the Ahsap continued to listen to her, 'then they must have come here for a reason.'

'A reason!' . . . 'What reason?' . . . 'Have you ever heard anything more—'

The Ahsap raised a hand sharply. The counsellors glared.

'What should I do about it, if they have a . . . reason?' said the Ahsap quietly.

'You should find out what it is,' said the counsellor.

At this the other counsellors did not shout, or stamp, or push, or jostle. They stared wide-eyed, open-mouthed, struck dumb by disbelief. The *Ahsap* should find out? The Ahsap did not speak to prisoners. Prule did that, or, if it was absolutely necessary—a matter of the *gravest* urgency—one of the counsellors might do it. But the Ahsap? If the Ahsap were to start doing every little job for himself, it would hardly be worth having counsellors at all!

'But Ahsap . . .' said the oldest counsellor. He was the most cunning, the most clever, and knew the Ahsap's personality better than anyone else. 'This does not really *interest* you. You don't want to waste your time talking to a couple of prisoners. They won't have any clever ideas to discuss. After all, they were silly enough to let themselves be captured!'

'Yes,' said the Ahsap, 'you're probably right.' He looked back at the youngest counsellor. 'But *you* say I should find out their reasons.'

The youngest counsellor nodded, even though all the others were staring at her as fiercely as they could.

The Ahsap thought. The counsellors watched him, wondering what he would decide to do.

'Oh, I don't know,' said the Ahsap eventually. 'I don't really know if it does interest me enough.' He folded his arms, and gazed at the twinkling roof of his counsel chamber. Perhaps it *would* be interesting to speak to a couple of Overgrounders, he thought. But on the other hand, he could barely remember the last time he had a truly enjoyable conversation with an Overgrounder. They never seemed to be able to talk about anything but the sun, and how much they missed it.

The Ahsap sighed. It *would* be easy enough just to forget about them. After all, he could rely on Prule to send someone if there was anything he needed to know.

Chʌpter 14

'Prule,' said Bartlett, 'there is *one* thing that's still puzzling me.'

'Of course,' said Prule, 'people are always puzzled when they first arrive. Have some more fish.'

Prule offered Bartlett a bowl containing a whole heap of little fried fish. Three days had passed since Avner had brought them to the Underground, and food was delivered regularly by someone who knocked at Prule's door. Every meal seemed to consist of fish and platefuls of a chewy vegetable which was something like a cross between a lettuce and a sponge, which they called chinips. The fish, apparently, lived in the deep pools of the Underground, which was where the chinips grew as well.

'No thanks,' said Bartlett.

Jacques took a whole fistful of the fish and put them in his mouth. If the Ahsap

hadn't come for them within a week, Jacques had decided, he and Bartlett were going to break out of Prule's room. He was sure they could find their way back to the entrance to the Underground, and even if they had to fight and got recaptured on the way, that would probably just bring them to the attention of the Ahsap even quicker. 'On the other hand,' Bartlett had whispered to him while Prule was asleep, 'they may just bring us back and lock us up in that extra little room over there. That wouldn't improve things, would it?' Jacques had to admit that Bartlett was right, which was why he was prepared to wait a week. Otherwise, he would have tried to break out already!

'The thing is,' said Bartlett to Prule, as Jacques munched his fish, 'I don't really understand why we were meant to have a choice about being captured. I mean, why didn't you just take us anyway? And why didn't you take us when we were wandering around the first time? You wouldn't have had any problem. And for that matter, why don't you just capture the guards whenever they arrive and start—'

'Why? Why? Why?' cried Prule, throwing his head back with laughter. 'It's very simple,' he said when he had recovered, pulling the wisps of his beard out of his eyebrows, 'we never capture anyone when they're on the stonefields.'

'Why not?'

'It's a secret,' said Prule craftily. 'Why don't you tell me yours, and I'll tell you mine.'

'Prule, it is *not* a secret. I don't believe you for one second. Besides, I've told you a thousand times already, I can only tell the Ahsap why we're here.'

'You're a stubborn man, Bartlett,' said Prule. 'Perhaps you *should* tell me. Then, if it's a really good reason, if it really would interest him, I could let the Ahsap know. You've already waited three days. He's probably lost interest. I told you, he often does.'

Jacques glanced at Bartlett and raised an eyebrow. Why not? Bartlett considered. It was a risk to tell Prule unless there was absolutely no other way. If Prule thought the Ahsap would be interested, everything would be all right—but what if Prule thought the Ahsap *wouldn't* be interested? He'd probably send someone to tell the Ahsap not to bother. If that happened, the only way out would be Jacques' escape plan—which would almost certainly end with both of them being locked up in Prule's extra room. After all, even if they managed to get out into the stonefields again, how would they escape? The Undergrounders saw everything. They would easily find them and capture them once more.

'Well?' said Prule. He raised his eyebrows, and nodded encouragingly, as if to show how easy it would be for Bartlett to tell him. 'You don't want to leave it too long, you know.'

Bartlett thought for a moment longer. He shook his head.

'All right,' said Prule, when they had finished eating, 'since you've asked, I'll tell you why we don't capture people on the stonefields. It's perfectly simple, you could probably work it out for yourself anyway. In the Overground, they don't really know for sure that we exist. You see, we *know* that. And even the ones that do believe in us, don't know where we are. They only *think* we're in the stonefields, because they can't imagine anywhere else we could be. Overgrounders aren't really very clever, you know. Oops! Sorry. I'm not talking about you, Bartlett. Or you, Jacques. But they aren't, you know, in general. So, what do you think would happen if everyone who came into the stonefields disappeared? They'd know for sure that we're here! That's why we have an iron rule: NO ONE GETS CAPTURED IN THE STONEFIELDS.'

'But you captured *us*.'

'You were the exception. Even iron bends.'

Bartlett laughed.

'Yes,' said Prule, 'I thought that was quite clever myself. Come on, Jacques, give us a smile.'

Jacques nodded and grinned for the old man. It *was* quite clever, for a Prule.

'That's better. Anyway,' said Prule, 'we gave you a choice, remember? We didn't really want to capture you. In fact, we don't want to capture people at all. What would we want them for? *They* don't want to be here and *we* don't want to have them. More trouble than they're worth. I've had people locked up here for months—months—before they're ready to come out. Bawling and screaming, scratching and biting every time you bring them out. And why? Just because they miss the sun. Is that reasonable? The *sun!* After all, what's so special about it? *Everyone* in the Overground has it. How precious can it be?'

'It is quite precious, Prule,' said Bartlett.

Prule shrugged. 'Suit yourself.' He scratched his chin through his beard. 'No, we don't want people. Goats! It's goats we want. Wonderful animals. Sheep don't last a month down here. Just sit down on their knees and pine away. And once one of them sits down, the whole lot do it! But goats—goats find their feet in no time. They love the rock. They scramble around, you can't imagine! And the best thing about them is—they'll eat chinips!' Prule nodded his head, smiling to himself. 'Wonderful, intelligent animals.'

'So that's what you take?'

'Only when we need them. You see, there is one problem with goats: down here, they don't have many kids. No one knows why. So every so often, we have to go and get some more. Is that too much to ask? They're all we have down here, apart from fish and chinips. And in the Overground, you have everything else, including your precious sun. But *people*? No, it's only when people get in the way that we take them. It's the goats we want.'

Bartlett frowned. He glanced at Jacques. Was this true?

101

Sol said that sheer envy drove them to kidnap people, that they made them slaves, prisoners. Wasn't Prule making it all sound just a *little* bit better than it really was?

'Slaves?' said Prule. '*Prisoners?* Nonsense! They live just like any of us, as much fish and chinips as they can eat. If you don't believe me, it won't be long before you see for yourself.'

'What about the Pasha's boy, then?' said Bartlett. 'What about *him*?'

Prule narrowed his eyes. 'What do you know about the Pasha's boy?'

'Don't tell me *he* got in the way.'

'Do you think we wanted the Pasha's boy?'

'Why else did you take him?'

'Are you *crazy?* Ever since we took him they've had ten times as many guards on the stonefields as they had before. It's all we can do just to keep our eyes on them. I'll tell you what happened with the Pasha's boy! He was in the middle of the country. What was he doing there? Having a stroll in the middle of the night. Why wasn't he asleep like any other boy? And what do you think happened when he just decided to get up and go for a stroll in the middle of the night?'

Bartlett and Jacques stared, open-mouthed, waiting to find out.

'He walked straight into a herd of goats we were taking! Six of our men were there, bringing the goats back during the night. A brilliant operation. A perfect plan. Except for this one boy who had to walk into the middle of it and spoil everything!'

Prule leaned back against the wall, breathing heavily.

'But why did they have to take him?' said Bartlett.

'We have an iron rule, Bartlett, just like the other one. Why do you think the Overgrounders aren't sure if we exist? Why do you think they've never been able to follow us and find out where we live? I'll tell you why: "A PERSON GETS CAPTURED IF HE SEES YOU TAKING GOATS."'

'Even iron bends,' whispered Bartlett.

Prule sighed. 'I wish they'd bent it. But who knew, Bartlett? Who knew who he was? It wasn't until they got back here that anyone found out. *Then* the boy pipes up. What happened to his voice before that? "I'm the Pasha's son," he says, "and you're all in trouble." In this very room, Bartlett. In this very room!'

Prule looked around the room, as if the echo of the boy's voice could still be heard.

'It was too late. If only he'd spoken sooner.'

'Someone could have asked.'

Prule waved his hand. 'It was impossible to send him back—he would have told all our secrets. They would have known where we were, how to find us. They would have come to destroy us!'

'Maybe they wouldn't want to destroy you if you hadn't made yourselves their enemies,' said Bartlett.

'Made ourselves *their* enemies? We didn't make ourselves their enemies—they made themselves *ours!* Listen, have you stopped to ask why we live here under the ground? Our people came here centuries ago. There were not many of them. They were escaping from another country. They walked through caves, for weeks, for months.'

'The Margoulis Caverns?'

'Yes, the Margoulis Caverns. They were fleeing— What's wrong?' said Prule, noticing the look of dismay that came over both Bartlett and Jacques as he said it.

'Well . . . it's just . . . we thought *we* were the first ones to explore the Margoulis Caverns.'

Prule laughed. 'How can anyone ever be sure they're the first person to do *anything*? Anyway, these people weren't exploring, Bartlett. They were fleeing for their lives! Many died, but a few survived. But eventually, when they came out of the caves, and found their way out of the stonefields, what happened? The people who lived on the grasslands didn't want them either. They drove them back towards the caves. So what could they do? Behind them were the Margoulis Caverns, and at the other end of that, their old enemies. In front of them were new enemies. And there, in the stonefields, how could they live? But there was one thing they *had* learned, probably better than anyone else in the world: to survive under the ground. They'd done if for months. So that's what they did. Here we made our home—dug it, carved it, hollowed it out, shaped it with our own hands. Generation after generation. That's how we survived. We left the sun for others.' Prule paused. He gazed into his beard. 'Only goats,' he murmured. 'If not for the goats, we would need to have nothing to do with the Overgrounders.'

Bartlett frowned. Each side thought the other was its enemy—and therefore, each had become the enemy of the other. Who knew what the truth had been, centuries before?

'The Pasha's son? It's the worst thing that's happened to us in years,' Prule said. He leaned his head against the wall and closed his eyes.

Suddenly he opened them again.

'Why all these questions about the Pasha's son?' He smiled craftily. 'That's it, isn't it? That's why you're here.'

'Prule, I told you, I can't—'

'We have another iron rule, Bartlett, the third and last: NO ONE WHO HAS BEEN CAPTURED EVER—'

'Prule, I think we know what that rule is.'

'Yes, but Bartlett, the thing is . . . Listen, I'm just trying to help. Let me ask you a question. You haven't come to try to get the Pasha's son back, have you?'

'What if we have?'

Prule shook his head. 'Bartlett, the Ahsap's not going to be interested in that! I think he'd . . . I think he'd just laugh! We all would.'

And it was true, at least for Prule, because even as he spoke he was struggling to stay serious, and a moment later he flipped his head back and was giggling into his beard, which covered his whole face.

Bartlett glanced at Jacques. Jacques crossed his arms across his chest, not uttering a word.

'I'm sorry,' said Prule, when he had recovered. 'I couldn't help myself. Listen, Bartlett, can't you think of something else? What about telling the Ahsap you've got some poems to tell him? He might like that. Of course, you'd have to make a couple up, but I could help you. But I can't possibly send someone to tell him you want the Pasha's boy. For a start, the Ahsap wouldn't *believe* anything so preposterous. And secondly—'

There was a knock on the door.

Prule looked at Bartlett and Jacques in surprise. 'Who can that be? You aren't expecting visitors, are you?'

Chapter 15

The long, wide corridor that led from the entrance to the Underground ran far into the distance, as straight as an arrow. Avner had brought Bartlett and Jacques back to it from Prule's chamber, and now they were following it once more, moving towards the heart of the Underground. Ahead of them, the flames of the oil lamps flickered in two long lines.

As they walked, people came from other tunnels to watch them pass. Some of them began to follow, and this time Avner said nothing to stop them.

'They've all heard,' he explained to Bartlett and Jacques.

'What?'

'You'll see,' said Avner, and he grinned mischievously.

Soon there was a whole procession marching along the corridor: Avner at the front, then Bartlett and Jacques, then a crowd of the Undergrounders in their goat-skin clothes, some of them carrying big bunches of chinips and munching as they went along. Goats pranced amongst the people as well. The flames danced and wavered as the procession passed. The walls of the passage echoed with the sound of voices, the bleats of goats, the noise of marching feet.

Bartlett looked around at the curious, excited faces behind him, lit up by the flames. He caught Jacques' eye and grinned.

Finally Avner stopped. The long corridor had come to an end, and there was a door in front of them. A single large lamp burned above it.

The crowd fell silent.

Avner turned to Bartlett. 'It's a very great honour, you know,' he said seriously, 'for the Ahsap to ask to see you. Of course, after I captured you, he asked to see *me*, but that's hardly a surprise.'

'Really?'

'Well, it was a *bit* of a surprise,' Avner said.

'You do exaggerate sometimes, don't you, Avner?' said Bartlett.

'Hardly ever!' cried Avner, exaggerating, and looking around to see if anyone else in the crowd had heard. Then his face became serious again, he turned back, put his hand on the door handle, and opened the door.

Bartlett and Jacques gazed in wonder at the room. Its polished walls glistened as if they were made of glass. Tiny lamps twinkled in the roof, casting glinting lights into the water of a pool, as if a starlit sky were reflected in the sea. And on the other side of the pool, directly opposite the door, between two curving and crowded benches, sat someone on a beautifully carved throne of rock, someone, Bartlett and Jacques immediately realised, who could only be one person: the multiplier of four digit numbers, the composer of silly poems . . . the Ahsap.

The Ahsap was considering them gravely. The people sitting on the benches on either side of him were fidgeting restlessly. It looked like they could hardly bear to stay in their seats. Bartlett noticed the Ahsap glance at them in exasperation once or twice before he spoke.

'You have been here now for three days?' he said finally, without any introductions.

Bartlett nodded. 'Four, if you count the day they brought us.'

'I brought them myself, Ahsap,' said Avner, in case the Ahsap had forgotten.

'Quiet, Avner.' He looked at Bartlett again. 'We don't do that here. We don't count the day you were brought in. Or do we?' he suddenly asked, turning to one of his counsellors.

'No, we don't, Ahsap,' whispered the counsellor.

'Yes we do!' shouted another.

'No we don't!' shouted the first.

'We do!' . . . *'We don't!'* . . . *'We do!'* . . . One of the counsellors was already on his feet, and another three were getting ready to launch themselves.

'Enough! E—*nough!'* cried the Ahsap.

The counsellors stopped abruptly. They sat down again, glaring at each other.

'It doesn't really matter whether it's three days or four,' said Bartlett helpfully.

The Ahsap looked up. 'No,' he said gratefully, 'I'm glad you agree.'

'What does matter is *why* we're here.'

There was silence. Every one of the counsellors was still, even the most fidgety. They stared, waiting to find out.

'Yes,' said the Ahsap. 'I couldn't decide whether it would be interesting or not. I can't be bothered with things that aren't interesting.' He waved a hand towards his counsellors. 'They bring me enough of that already.'

'I'm sure you'll be interested,' said Bartlett.

'Yes, that's what *she* said,' replied the Ahsap, indicating the youngest counsellor at the far end of one of the benches. But then he pointed to the oldest counsellor who was sitting right next to him. '*He* said I wouldn't be.'

'Well, I'm glad you believed her.'

'No,' said the Ahsap, 'I didn't know who to believe. It's just that *he* kept telling me I wouldn't be interested, so often, so repetitively, that I couldn't stop thinking about it! If he'd only kept quiet I might have forgotten about it forever.'

Bartlett grinned. The oldest counsellor looked away foolishly.

'So,' said the Ahsap, 'let's see who's right.' He narrowed his eyes. 'Why did you ask to be captured? Is it because you're mad?'

Bartlett shook his head.

'See, Ahsap?' cried Avner. 'I told you. And they're not stupid either!'

'Avner, if you don't be quiet I'll have to send you out.'

'Sorry, Ahsap. I'm very sorry . . . Sorry . . . Ahsap . . .'

The Ahsap sighed. 'So, you're not mad and you're not stupid. Why *are* you here?'

Bartlett glanced at Jacques for an instant. Then he turned back to face the Ahsap and his counsellors. He took a deep breath.

'We've come for the Pasha's son.'

Bartlett and Jacques watched in amazement. A riot had broken out on the other side of the pool. The counsellors were on their feet, jumping and stamping, pushing and shoving, pointing and shouting, all trying to get the Ahsap's attention. Their cries echoed off the stone roof of the chamber and bounced around the walls. *'The Pasha's son!'* . . . *'They want him!'* . . . *'They can't have him!'* . . .

Only two people remained in their seats: the Ahsap, who had buried his face in his hands, and the youngest of the counsellors, sitting at the very end of the bench on the Ahsap's left.

The counsellors were working themselves into a frenzy, leaping on top of each other to get closer to the Ahsap. *'Whip them!'* . . . *'Trip them!'* . . . *'Beat them!'* . . . *'Eat them!'* . . . *'Roast them'* . . . *'Toast—'*

There was a splash.

The Ahsap looked up with a start. Suddenly everyone was silent. They glanced guiltily at the Ahsap. The Ahsap, they knew, hated seeing his counsellors fall into the pool, especially when other people were watching. It was so embarrassing: he hated it more than anything else in the world.

The counsellor in the pool was thrashing wildly. It looked like he might drown while the others stood by, too scared to move.

'Help him out,' hissed the Ahsap.

They all rushed forward.

'One of you. Just one!'

The counsellors froze. The one nearest the pool leaned over and caught the arms waving in the water. The other counsellor clambered out, not daring to look the Ahsap in the eye.

'Sit down, all of you.'

The counsellors sat down. The one who had fallen into the pool was soaking. The ones who sat next to him pushed up against their neighbours, trying to keep themselves dry. Their neighbours pushed up against *their* neighbours. Finally everyone on the bench was pushing and elbowing one way or the other. The Ahsap watched in despair. The counsellors on the other bench grinned at the discomfort of their colleagues. The pushing went on for five minutes.

A puddle of water was collecting on the ground under the soaked counsellor.

Finally, the Ahsap cleared his throat, trying to ignore the occasional shove and yelp that still came from the bench. 'Now,' he said, looking at Bartlett and Jacques le Grand once more, 'that was a very foolish thing you just said, and even though I don't think people need to go diving into the water because of it . . .' he glared for a moment at the wet counsellor, who looked away quickly, shivering, 'you ought to have known better than to say it.'

'Why?' said Bartlett.

'Because Prule should have told you we don't send people back. That's one of Prule's jobs. Don't tell me he didn't do it.'

'He did tell us.'

'Exactly,' said the Ahsap. 'And that's why you should have known better than to say what you did. It's preposterous!'

'Prule also told us you sometimes bend the rules,' said Bartlett.

'He told you that? Well, that *isn't* his job.' The Ahsap leaned towards his nearest counsellor: 'Remind me to have a word about that with Prule next time I see him.'

Jacques glanced at Bartlett. They weren't here to talk about Prule!

Bartlett took a step forward. He was standing at the very edge of the pool. 'Ahsap, we've come for the Pasha's son.'

The counsellors gasped again. The Ahsap raised a finger sternly in the air, and this, together with the sound of chattering teeth that came from the one who had fallen in last time, somehow kept them in their seats.

The Ahsap leaned forward, peering at Bartlett, frowning.

'Where do you come from? Are you from the Pasha?'

'No.'

'Then why do you want his son? What will you do with him?'

'Give him back.'

'Why?'

'Does it matter why we want to give him back?' said Bartlett. 'Wouldn't you rather hear why you should return him?'

The Ahsap laughed. The counsellors laughed as well,

giggling and wheezing. Only the youngest one remained silent, watching Bartlett and Jacques thoughtfully.

'Why *I* should want to return him?' said the Ahsap eventually. 'Give me one good reason.'

'I will give you four.'

'Oh, four!' cried the Ahsap. 'This will be four times as funny.'

'First,' said Bartlett, sticking out his thumb, 'because the boy is of no use to you.'

'*They* are of no use to me!' cried the Ahsap, flinging his arm out to indicate his counsellors, 'but I do not send them to the Overground.'

The counsellors frowned. They didn't find that particularly funny.

'Second,' said Bartlett, sticking out his index finger, 'the Pasha's guards are in the stonefields all the time, looking for him, which makes life difficult for your people.'

'My people can manage.'

'Third,' said Bartlett, sticking out his next finger, 'the boy could never lead the Pasha's guards back to you. He came at night and could never find the way back.'

'He won't need to find the way back because he isn't *going* back.'

'Fourth,' said Bartlett . . .

'This had better be good,' said the Ahsap, rubbing his hands, 'the other three were rubbish.'

'Fourth,' repeated Bartlett, sticking out his fourth finger, 'because the Pasha will be grateful, and perhaps, instead of hiding from each other, you can learn to live together openly. Instead of stealing goats, you can trade fish and chinips for them.'

'Oh, yes, that's the best yet. Listen, we *like* to steal goats! I write *poems* about stealing goats!' The Ahsap slapped his thighs and roared with laughter, and the counsellors, thinking it was safe, slapped their thighs and roared *'It's true! . . . He does!'* until the Ahsap raised his finger again to tell them to stop.

'Is that all?' said the Ahsap.

The smile lingered on the Ahsap's face. The counsellors grinned mockingly. The four reasons, which Bartlett and Jacques had worked out together one night while Prule slept, were not enough! The Ahsap was going to refuse them. And if he refused them, they would be trapped forever in the Underground, and Gozo would remain forever locked in the Pasha's palace.

Desperation! Bartlett's mind raced. There were only minutes, perhaps seconds left. The counsellors grinned. The Ahsap smiled. How much longer would he wait? This was their only opportunity. If the Ahsap sent them away, they would never be summoned again. But what else could he say? He glanced at Jacques. How else could he persuade the Ahsap?

Suddenly Bartlett knew. *He* couldn't tell what would persuade the Ahsap—only the Ahsap himself could tell what that was!

'No,' said Bartlett, turning back to the Ahsap, 'that's not all. There's a fifth reason. I was keeping it for last.'

'Excellent!' cried the Ahsap, 'You should have said so before. I can do with another joke. What is it?'

'This: In return for the Pasha's son, we will bring you whatever you ask for.'

The Ahsap grinned. 'You don't expect me to believe that!'

Bartlett shrugged. He tried to make it look as if it didn't make the slightest bit of difference to *him* whether the Ahsap believed it or not. In this kind of situation, Bartlett knew, the less certain you are, the less uncertainty you can afford to show.

'We will bring you whatever you ask for,' he repeated. 'If you don't believe us, you will never know whether we could have got it for you or not.'

The Ahsap glanced at Jacques le Grand. Jacques nodded his head solemnly, hoping it would look as if he had some idea what Bartlett was talking about.

The counsellors fidgeted, murmuring, itching to jump up and shout for the Ahsap's attention. But the Ahsap was silent. Finally he turned and looked at the youngest counsellor, who was sitting in the most distant chair.

'What do you think?'

'Ahsap!' . . . *'Her?'* . . . *'Not again!'*

'Quiet! Qui—*et!* Now,' said the Ahsap to the youngest counsellor once more, 'what do you think?'

'Ahsap, I don't know if anyone can bring you—'

'See?' . . . *'She doesn't know!'* . . . *'No idea!'* . . .

'Quiet, I said!'

The youngest counsellor continued. 'I don't know if

anyone can bring you whatever you ask for. But I agree with the strangers' second reason. The Pasha's guards are everywhere. Since we took the boy, there are more than there ever were before. Soon we won't be able to watch them all. And they'll be everywhere for years unless we give the boy back.'

The Ahsap frowned.

'And besides, perhaps we *can* live openly with the Overgrounders, and give them fish instead of stealing their goats.'

'*Give them fish?*' . . . '*Stop stealing goats?*' The counsellors shouted from their benches, their voices growing louder and louder, while the Ahsap remained silent, deep in thought. Suddenly he jumped out of his chair. He *never* did that. The counsellors fell silent at the sight.

'You are a very adventurous man, Bartlett,' he said, pacing up and down in front of the counsellors' benches. 'Yes, very adventurous. The way you allowed yourself to be captured shows that.'

Bartlett shrugged. 'It's not just me, Ahsap. Jacques is just as adventurous.'

'So—I have decided to let you go . . .'

The counsellors gasped. '*Ahsap!*' cried one.

The Ahsap raised his finger. 'I will let you go, Bartlett, you and Jacques. Prule is quite right—the rules are mine and I am allowed to bend them. But I will *not* give you the Pasha's son. Not yet. You said you will bring whatever I ask for. First come back with that—*then* I will give you the boy.'

118

'All right,' said Bartlett, 'but we have to see him first.'

'You can't see him!' said the Ahsap. 'Why should you? If you don't succeed, you won't be taking him.'

'If we don't see him first, we don't go.'

The Ahsap gazed at Bartlett, narrowing his eyes. 'All right. You can see him, but you can't talk to him.'

Now it was Bartlett's turn to consider. Finally he nodded.

'Good,' said the Ahsap. He crossed his arms. 'I suppose you'll want to know what it is you have to bring me.'

'It would help,' said Bartlett.

The Ahsap smiled. 'What is it that the Overgrounders call their city? The City of Sun, isn't it? Tell me, why do they call it that?'

Bartlett shrugged. 'I suppose . . . Their city is made out of white stone, and when the sun shines, it's very bright. The stone reflects the sunlight. In fact, it's almost like looking at the sun itself.'

'Is it?' said the Ahsap. 'Well, here we have no sun. Here we must make do with something else. Look around you, Bartlett. If it is the City of Sun that the Overgrounders have . . . then *this* is the City of Flames!'

The Ahsap paused. In the chamber, there was not a sound, not a breath. Bartlett, Jacques, the counsellors, all looked around, gazing at the flames of the lamps on the walls, the twinkling starspots in the ceiling. The walls glowed red like crystal embers, the water in the pool twinkled with lights. If there had been a single, tiny fish in that pool, you could have heard it swimming.

119

'Now, think, Bartlett: can't you guess what you must bring?'

Bartlett looked back at the Ahsap.

'The sun.'

The Ahsap spread his arms wide, as if to hold within them the counsellors around him, the water in the pool, the rock of the walls, the caverns and the corridors and the very lives of the people who lived within them.

'Bring the sun to the City of Flames, Bartlett—and the boy is yours!'

Chapter 16

Avner, Bartlett and Jacques stood at the opening of a tunnel, high in the wall of a gigantic cavern. Steps ran down to the bottom, where there was an enormous, dark pool. Two lamps burned above the water, and the light was dim. As the flames flickered, veins of crystal in the walls glittered and sparkled.

At the foot of the steps, two figures stood in the shadows.

'No further,' said Avner. He pointed at one of the figures beside the pool. 'There he is. No talking to him. The Ahsap said, remember?'

Bartlett and Jacques peered downwards. One of the figures was larger than the other, and he was holding a net. He was showing the smaller one how to use it. As they watched, the smaller figure took the net and tried to throw it in. The larger one shook his head, hauled the net in, and began to talk to him once more.

'He's teaching him to fish,' said Avner. He laughed softly. 'He's not very good, but he'll learn.'

Bartlett peered down at the pool. Was it the Pasha's son? It was difficult to see. He was in shadow. He was the right size—but lots of boys would be the right size. Bartlett glanced at Jacques. Jacques shrugged. He couldn't tell either.

'I can't see from here,' said Bartlett.

Avner shrugged. 'No closer. The Ahsap said.'

'I'm sorry, Avner, but unless I can be sure—'

Suddenly the boy swung the net again. His face turned up. For an instant, it moved into the light.

'Gozo!' cried Bartlett, before he could even think what he was saying.

The boy heard. The net went limp in his hand. A puzzled expression came across his face. The name Gozo meant nothing to him. But he continued to look up, staring at the three people who had suddenly appeared above him, as if he knew that they had come for a reason, that something special was happening, something that concerned him.

It *was* the same face, the same upturned nose, the same spiky hair. He could have been sitting on a wagon with a load of melidrops behind him.

Jacques nodded. He almost expected to hear the boy cry out 'Mr Bartlett!' in excitement.

But the boy did not cry out. He gazed silently, and a moment later, the other figure took his arm and turned him away.

'Well?' said Avner.

Bartlett nodded.

Avner turned back into the passage. Jacques followed him. But for a moment Bartlett could not draw himself away. He continued to watch the figures in the shadows below him. The man was talking to the boy again, holding out the net and showing him, with the movement of his arm, how it should be spread. The boy took the net and threw it once more. But his movements were slow and leaden, there was no energy in them, no spark.

There was no joy left in the boy. Bartlett could see it even from that distance, even in that darkness. When did he last smile? The shadows had driven all his brightness away.

He slung the net again, without interest or will.

The net hit the water with barely a ripple.

'Darian . . .' Bartlett whispered. No one could hear him but himself. 'I will be back for you.'

Chapter 17

The sun! It streamed over them, stabbing them with its light, warming them with its heat. They blinked, screwed up their eyes, shielded their faces with their hands. And yet they turned towards it, towards the great burning disc of the sun, as a thirsty person turns towards drink, a hungry person towards food. The sun was golden, and the touch of it upon their skin once more was sweeter than honey.

Avner, sheltering in the shadow of the pillar, watched them with curiosity. Overgrounders were very strange, he thought. He had brought them back along the corridor to the steps and with a movement too quick for Bartlett to follow, had opened the entrance above their heads. Then they emerged into the valley of rock where the sun awaited them.

'Can you find your way out of the stonefields?' asked Avner.

Bartlett nodded.

'If you get lost, don't worry. Just sit down again. We'll know you need help.'

'How will you know we're sitting?'

Avner laughed. 'We'll be watching, Bartlett.'

'And when we come back?'

'*Are* you coming back? People are saying you tricked the Ahsap, Bartlett, that you offered him gold and diamonds, goats and herrings.'

'Avner, stop exaggerating. You heard exactly what we offered him, and that's what we'll bring when we come back.'

'Well, we'll be watching. We'll know when you've arrived.'

Bartlett nodded. 'We'll see you then, Avner.'

Avner didn't look convinced. He watched them walk away. They went past a clump of boulders and disappeared. Then Avner dropped down the steps. An instant later, the pillar moved. Suddenly the valley of rock was empty again, silent, as if no human being had ever set foot upon its surface.

Jacques marched steadily over the stone, his eyes fixed ahead, his lips tightly pressed together. Pebbles flew from under his boots.

'I know,' said Bartlett.

What? What did he know?

'We were going to give him four reasons. We agreed. I know. But Jacques, he wasn't going to let us go! He wasn't going to do it. What else could I do?'

But that wasn't the problem, that wasn't it at all. Jacques would have done the same himself. He would have given a sixth reason, and a seventh, and an eighth if necessary, and then thrown in a ninth reason just for good measure. The number of reasons had nothing to do with it.

He continued marching. He set a furious pace. When Jacques chose to march quickly, Bartlett almost had to run to keep up.

Suddenly Jacques stopped. He gazed deep into Bartlett's eyes, a powerful frown on his face. 'You actually want us to try, don't you?'

For a moment Bartlett stared back at him. Then he broke into a sheepish grin.

But Jacques simply shook his head in disbelief. 'No, you actually *want* us to try. Well, I prefer to try things that are at least possible. Give me a five percent chance, a one percent chance, and I'll try. I'll give everything I have, you know that. But things that are impossible? No, it makes no sense.'

This was turning into quite a speech for Jacques! It was always eerie when Jacques decided to make a speech, and here, on top of a hill in the stonefields, he couldn't have chosen an eerier place to do it.

'What would Sutton Pufrock say about an explorer who tries the impossible? We both know, don't we?'

'That he's taking one journey too many,' murmured Bartlett.

Jacques nodded. 'Look, why don't we just steal the maps from the Pasha's palace?'

'Do we still want the maps?'

Jacques gave Bartlett a look of fierce determination. Of course they still wanted the maps! What difference did it make if a group of people had passed through the Margoulis Caverns centuries before them? They weren't exploring, they wouldn't have investigated every corner and cranny. And they hadn't mapped it all!

'We'll try to snatch Gozo as well,' said Jacques. 'I bet it wouldn't take us more than ten minutes to get those bars off his window. Then we just have to get away. It mightn't be easy, we mightn't succeed—but at least we'd have a chance!'

Bartlett sighed. 'And the boy, Jacques?'

Jacques shook his head. 'The sun, Bartlett? To bring the *sun?*'

'You know what Sutton Pufrock would say, don't you?'

Jacques raised an eyebrow.

'He'd say, "Don't say something's impossible until you're sure you've thought of every possibility."'

Jacques frowned. Half of the time Bartlett just made up Sutton Pufrock's 'sayings' himself, he was sure. 'And what possibility haven't we thought of?'

'I don't know,' said Bartlett. 'But we might have missed something. *That's* a possibility.'

'Bring the sun, Bartlett? What does it even mean?'

'What does it mean?' Bartlett gazed up at the sky. 'What does it *mean. . .?*' he repeated, wondering. Then he looked back and shrugged. 'We're not going to find out here.'

They weren't going to find out anywhere. There was nothing *to* find out.

'All right. I'll tell you what we'll do,' said Bartlett, as they started to walk again. 'We'll go back to the Pasha's city, and if we can't think of anything by the time we get there, we'll do what you say. We'll try to get Gozo and the maps and get away.'

'Really?' said Jacques, 'as simple as that?'

'As simple as that,' said Bartlett—and then, of course, they'd just have to find a way of getting Darian as well!

Chapter 18

'For the last time, what are these *maps?*' demanded the Pasha, holding up one of the scrolls from Jacques le Grand's bag.

Gozo rolled his eyes. 'I've told you already, the Margoulis Caverns.'

'The Underground?'

'No, not the Underground. I don't know anything about the Underground. Why do you keep asking? I've told you a hundred times—'

'Darian . . .'

'And I'm not *Darian!* I've told you that a hundred times as well!' cried Gozo excitedly, and he jumped up and down in frustration.

The Pasha, in turn, jumped to *his* feet. 'When will you stop pretending? What did they do to you there in the Underground? Now, you listen to me—'

'You listen to *me!*' cried Gozo.

'You listen to me *first!*' roared the Pasha. 'I'm asking you a simple question: What are these maps? Why won't you show us where we can get into the Underground? Don't you care about the others who are there? Now, *what are these—*'

'Sit down, dear,' said the Pashanne.

The Pasha's face was red, his chest heaving with anger. He sat down, still glaring at Gozo.

'Now, Darian . . .' said the Pashanne.

'I'm not Darian and I'm not going to answer that name any more. Call me Gozo or call me nothing.'

'All right, Nothing,' said the Pasha. 'Tell me what are these—'

'No, dear,' said the Pashanne, 'just be quiet, all right? Now, Darian . . .'

'Gozo!'

'If we can tell from those maps how to get to the Underground, then all our soldiers can go there. Then there won't be any Underground left. No one else will have to go through what you went through. Now, don't you want to tell us what these maps are?'

'I've told you,' said Gozo, 'what more do you want? They're the Margoulis Caverns.'

'These caverns again!' cried the Pasha, throwing his hands up in despair.

'Well, if you don't believe me, wait until Bartlett and Jacques come back. *They'll* tell you what they are! They'll tell you who I am, too.'

The Pasha laughed. 'Bartlett and Jacques? Do you really think they're coming back for you? They've run off.'

'No they haven't!'

'They've run off! They've run off!' repeated the Pasha cruelly. 'I should have hanged them when I had the chance.'

'Darian,' said the Pashanne, 'they're gone. It's a month since they left. They're not coming back.'

Gozo frowned.

The Pashanne reached out her arms. She pulled Gozo towards her and tried to hug him. 'You have to understand that, Darian. And you have to understand that all these . . . things, these things you imagine . . . these caverns, and this ship you told us about before that . . . and the ice voyage . . . you have to understand they're just your imagination. They're not real.'

'They *are* real!' cried Gozo, struggling to get out of the Pashanne's embrace. 'They're as real as you and me!'

And he broke away and ran out of the room, and into the corridor, and through the palace, where silk curtains billowed in front of the windows and shafts of moonlight fell across the floor, and he didn't stop until he came to his own room, where Mirta, the only person who believed him, was waiting.

Chapter 19

Gozo threw himself down on the bed. He didn't want to cry. He tried as hard as he could to stop the tears. But what if the Pasha were right? What if they were *never* coming back?

'Of course they're coming back,' said Mirta, stroking his head. 'Of course they are.'

'No, they're not. They're not!' cried Gozo in anguish.

'Now, Gozo,' said Mirta sternly, 'what is it you always tell me? An explorer has to have three things: Inventiveness, Desperation, and . . . ?'

Gozo kicked his legs and shrugged his shoulders.

'And?'

'Perseverance,' Gozo muttered.

'And didn't Bartlett tell you that himself, that you had to persevere? Well, is that what you're doing now? You can't give up. What would Bartlett do? He wouldn't give up, would he?'

Gozo shrugged.

'Would he?'

'No,' said Gozo.

'Exactly. Now, sit up and dry your eyes, and we'll play a game of marzipan draughts.'

'I wasn't crying!'

'Of course not, but dry your eyes anyway,' said Mirta, and she held out a big silk handkerchief, and when

Gozo wouldn't take it, she scrunched it up and rubbed it all over his face, and then she tweaked his nose, and pulled his ears, and pinched his cheeks, and messed his hair, with her quick darting hands, until he was screaming and giggling and twisting all over.

'Gozo!'

Gozo was shrieking so much, at first they didn't even hear Bartlett's voice.

Gozo ran to the window. Mirta followed him as quickly as she could.

'Mr Bartlett!' cried Gozo excitedly.

'Shhhh! We're not meant to be here.'

'Mr Bartlett, they said you were never coming back. And you too, Jacques!'

'And you believed them?'

'Never! Not for a minute! Not for a second!'

'Good,' said Bartlett. 'Now, we can't stay long . . .'

'Of course not,' said Mirta. 'You poor boys. It must be very uncomfortable hanging on to the bars out there.'

Jacques shrugged. He was examining the bars carefully, looking at the bolts that held them into the wall, picking at the cement to see if he could loosen them.

'Have you come to take me with you?' demanded Gozo, and he clapped his hands excitedly when he saw Jacques nod.

'Well,' said Bartlett, 'it's not quite as simple—'

'Mr Bartlett, I've had enough! I've eaten so much

marzipan I never want to see another piece again. And they keep asking me to show them how to get to the Underground. They want to take soldiers and destroy everything. And they never let me go out of the palace. And they never let me—'

'Gozo, we can't take you yet.'

Gozo frowned. 'Don't you want to take me?'

'Of course we want to take you,' said Bartlett. 'Why do you think we're here? It's just . . . we can't take you yet.'

'Why not?'

'We have to do something else first.'

'What?'

'We're not sure,' said Bartlett.

'You're not *sure*?'

'We're not sure *yet*,' said Bartlett. 'Listen, Gozo, we've seen the other boy—'

Mirta gasped, barely believing her ears.

'It's true,' said Bartlett. Now, we just have to work out how to get him back. Right, Jacques?'

Jacques raised an eyebrow. He started picking at the bolts again.

'Now, listen, Gozo, when we first met you, did we know how we were going to get the melidrop for the Queen? Did we?'

'No,' said Mirta, when Gozo refused to answer. He had told her the story a hundred times already. 'You thought you could use a wagon.'

'Exactly. And did we manage to do it in the end? Did we?'

'Yes,' muttered Gozo.

'And did the Queen wait?'

Gozo nodded.

'And she's the most impatient person in the world!' said Mirta. 'Remember, Gozo?'

'I remember! I remember everything! But Mr Bartlett—'

'Gozo, you have to wait. That's what we've come to tell you. Don't give up. Perseverance!'

'Not *more* Perseverance!'

Bartlett grinned. 'Yes, Gozo. *More* Perseverance.'

Gozo frowned. Mirta nudged him. 'All right, Mr Bartlett,' he mumbled eventually.

'Good,' said Bartlett. '*That's* what I wanted to hear. We'll be back, Gozo. Whatever anyone says, whatever anyone does, remember this: we *will* be back for you!'

'With Darian?' asked Mirta, her old eyes wide with hope.

'Of course,' said Bartlett, and he slipped away from the window, scrambling down the rough stones of the wall.

When they reached the bottom, the question was already in Jacques' eyes.

'I know, I know,' said Bartlett. 'If we couldn't think of anything by the time we got here, we were just going to take Gozo and get the maps. But I can't believe we've thought of everything. There must be *something*.

Something always turns up.'

No, sometimes something didn't turn up. Bartlett knew it himself.

'One more day, Jacques. Give me just one more day.'

Chapter 20

It was late. Sol's customers had all gone home. Bartlett and Jacques were sitting at a table by themselves. Sol had sent a boy to get More. The innkeeper himself was in his wine room, climbing on top of a barrel to reach a bottle of special wine. Sol liked to make himself comfortable when he knew he was going to hear a really fascinating story. He liked everything to be just right. He liked to have a cup of his finest wine in his hand, and to sip and sup it as he listened.

More arrived. Sol came out with the wine and filled their cups. Finally, everything was ready. He sat down, settled back in his chair, and took his first sip.

'Now,' he said, 'tell us about the Underground. Tell us how you got there, what you did, what you saw, who you met, what you heard, what you ate, when you left and how you got away. Tell us everything.'

Bartlett began to tell them. Sol and More listened to each word with concentration, unwilling to miss a single thing. The innkeeper leaned so far forward in his eagerness that his nose almost dipped into his wine cup. An hour must have gone by without a single interruption.

Suddenly Sol jerked upright and threw his arms up in disbelief. 'They don't want our people? Of course they want our people! They're our enemies. What else do they want?'

'Your goats.'

'Our goats? No, Bartlett, the goats just follow their masters.'

Bartlett shook his head.

'What about the Pasha's boy?'

'A mistake. He was the last person they wanted.'

Sol's eyes narrowed. He glanced at More. 'What do you think, More? Do you believe him?'

More shrugged. 'Where were they, Bartlett? Where did you find them?'

'I told you, they found us.'

'Yes, but where did they take you?'

Bartlett grinned. Sol was leaning further forward than ever, dying to find out. Bartlett didn't reply. He had no intention of telling. He wasn't going to let the Pasha send his army into the Underground.

'More wine, Jacques?' said Sol, pouring another cup.

Jacques didn't say anything either.

Sol sighed. Why was it that people always kept the best things to themselves? 'Tell us about it again, Bartlett. Tell us about the tunnels.'

'I've told you already.'

'Well, tell us about the old man, Prule.'

'I've told you all about him as well, Sol.'

'And chinips? Have you told us everything about those as well?'

Bartlett nodded.

Sol frowned. He wanted more. He always wanted more, he always wanted to hear new things, learn new facts, explore the whole world without having to leave the warmth of his inn. 'And now they want the sun,' he said, shaking his head in disbelief. 'First our goats, then our people, now our sun! Well, we're not going to give it to them! You're not planning to give them our sun, are you? Whose sun do you think it is? It doesn't belong—'

'Sol,' said Bartlett, '*what* are you talking about? Of course I'm not going to give them the sun. How could I? That's the whole problem, isn't it? The Ahsap won't give Darian back unless he gets the sun—and we have no idea how to give it to them.'

Sol sat back in his chair. More had a puzzled expression on his face, as if he were trying to work out how you could squeeze the sun into a tunnel in the Underground.

140

Sol picked up his cup and took another sip. His mind began to wander in and out of all the interesting facts that Bartlett had told them. He loved to let his mind wander like that, and Bartlett had given him so many new things to think about, so many fascinating tunnels and mysterious rooms into which his mind could wander and poke around . . .

'It's all upside down . . . and inside out,' he murmured, talking to himself as much as anyone else.

'What is?' asked Bartlett.

Sol looked up. 'The Underground. Don't you think? It's upside down. We build up—they dig down.' A puzzled smile came across Sol's lips. 'It's inside out. We raise walls around rooms—they hollow out rooms inside walls.'

'And it's back to front too!' said More. 'Their Ahsap is just Pasha written backwards.'

Everyone stared at More.

'Isn't it?' said More, gazing at them anxiously.

It *was*, that was the amazing thing.

Sol poured himself more wine and took a thoughtful sip. 'Yes, it's just as More says—it's all back to front. Their whole world is a reflection of ours. Those flames of theirs—what are they? Just a poor reflection of our sun! No wonder they want it.' Sol laughed. 'Maybe *all* their names are spelt backwards. What was the old man's name again. Prule? Elurp! What sort of a name is that? No, that's ridiculous. Sounds like some kind of goat-milk curd.'

'Or the sound you make when you're eating it,' said More, laughing.

'Exactly. Who else was there? Avner, wasn't that the other one's name, Bartlett? *Bartlett?*'

But Bartlett wasn't listening. He was staring at Jacques with a look of wild impatience on his face. Jacques knew that look. Inventiveness!

'The sun, Jacques,' Bartlett whispered.

Jacques frowned. What about the sun?

'We've got to get into the Pasha's palace.' Suddenly Bartlett turned to More. 'More, you've got to get us into the palace.'

'You don't want to see Gozo again, do you? What's wrong with the wall?'

Bartlett leapt up. The look of fierce urgency on his face left More speechless. 'The throne room, More. Get us into the throne room. Take us there—and the Ahsap will have his sun!'

Chapter 21

Bargus! Bargus was the one who could help them.

More shook his head. 'No, Bartlett, I don't think so. Bargus has changed since they let him into the Palace Guard. He thinks he's better than everyone else.'

But there was no alternative. As a Palace Guard, Bargus could move in and out of the palace freely. They could think of no one else who could get them into the throne room. Even Sol agreed.

But Bargus didn't. More convinced him to come to the inn late the next night, saying there was a very important matter he needed to discuss. Bargus stared at More angrily when he told him what he wanted.

'Do you think I joined the Palace Guard just to let people in when no one's looking? And people like that—*prisoners* that I captured! Sol, *you* should know better. I'm supposed to protect the Pasha, not help his enemies. Where are they, anyway?' Bargus demanded, jumping up and looking around the inn. They were nowhere to be seen. 'Why, if they were here right now, do you know what I'd do? I'd grab Bartlett by the neck in one hand, and as for Jacques le Grand, that big bully, that big bullock, that big . . . *person*, I'd . . . I'd—'

Jacques came out of the wine room, where he and Bartlett had been waiting.

Bargus stared.

Jacques stepped forward. Very softly, with one flick of his finger, he tipped Bargus' new orange turban—the one he'd been given when he joined the Palace Guard—off his head.

'I'd say: "Hello Jacques, very nice to see you again."'

Bartlett picked up the turban and handed it back to Bargus. 'You don't really want to grab me by the neck, do you, Bargus?'

'No, of course not. That was just a way of saying . . . I'd be so happy to see you . . . I'd hug you round the neck.'

'Well, I don't think we need to go that far,' said Bartlett. 'Why don't we all sit down?'

Bartlett waited. Bargus sat. He put his turban back on his head. His hands trembled so much that it slipped forwards on his nose. Everyone else sat down around the table.

'Now Bargus,' said Bartlett, 'you *are* going to have to help us. There's no alternative. You can do it for either of two reasons. First, because if you don't, Jacques and I are going to go to the Pasha and tell him what really happened when you "captured" us. I don't think the Pasha likes people who lie to get into the Palace Guard.'

'He doesn't,' said Sol, who always had an opinion.

'That's one reason. The second reason is that if you do help us, it means we'll be able to get the Pasha's son back. I think the Pasha *does* like people who help him get things he wants.'

'Definitely,' said Sol. 'Remember the man who brought him the recipe for Pomegranate Syllabub? He was so grateful he gave him an orchard.'

'A vineyard, Sol,' said More.

'No, it was an orchard.'

'It was a vineyard, wasn't it, Bargus?'

'What? Oh, I can't remember,' said Bargus, who didn't have time to think about things like that, with Jacques le Grand clenching his great fists and staring steadily at him from across the table.

'I'm telling you, Sol, it was an orchard,' said More. 'Not far from the Hatti Oasis.'

'It was nowhere *near* the Hatti Oasis!' cried Sol in disbelief. 'It was near the lakes.'

'It doesn't matter where it was,' said Bartlett.

'Of course it matters!' said Sol. 'All these years I've thought I knew where that orchard was, and now I find out the orchard's actually a vineyard? And it's near the Hatti Oasis? That matters, Bartlett. That matters a lot!'

'It doesn't matter *now*.'

'Oh,' said Sol, suddenly remembering why they were all there. 'You're right, it doesn't matter now.'

'Thank you.' Bartlett looked back at Bargus. 'Now, you can choose—'

'But it does matter another time. It does *matter*, Bartlett.'

Bartlett sighed, but he didn't take his eyes off Bargus. 'Now, Bargus, you can choose whichever of the reasons you like. It doesn't matter to us. But we need to get into

145

the Pasha's throne room, and you're the only one who can take us.'

Bargus frowned. Suddenly, he knew, everybody was staring at him again. He put his hands to his turban and tried to straighten it on his head.

Chapter 22

Late the following night, in an alley not far from the Pasha's palace, three figures slipped into the doorway of a house. It looked just like an ordinary doorway. Only the Palace Guards knew where it actually led. It was the opening of a secret passageway that had been created in case the Pasha ever needed to escape in secret. Three tunnels, five flights of steps, six rooms and fourteen doors from the alley entrance, Bargus, Bartlett and Jacques le Grand emerged in the courtyard of the palace.

The courtyard was deserted. The moon shone on it from a cloudless sky. They moved quickly through the shadow along the wall. Bargus took them through another door. Now they were inside the main building of the palace itself. Moonlight came through the windows, striping the floor with bars of light. Silk curtains billowed in the breeze. It was here, inside, that there was the greatest danger. They skipped rapidly from shadow to shadow, round corner after corner, through corridor after corridor.

Bargus led. He went round yet another corner in front of them.

'Who's that?'

Bartlett and Jacques froze. They pressed against the wall, in the deepest shadow they could find, trying to hear what was happening around the corner.

'Bargus? What are you doing here?'

There was silence. Bartlett could almost hear Bargus' mind working, trying to think of an explanation.

'I was just . . . going.'

'Where?'

'Back. I was just going back.'

'Forgot something?'

'Yes.'

'What?'

'What? Yes, what? My turban! I forgot my turban!'

'Bargus, it's on your head. You'll be forgetting that next!'

His turban? Couldn't he think of anything better? Who was going to believe that anyone could be so stupid? Now they were in trouble, now the other guard . . .

'Bargus, go to bed. When you wake up your turban will be just where you left it.'

There was laughter. The sound of footsteps. A dark figure crossed in front of them and moved away down the other passage.

Bargus' head appeared around the corner. 'Clever, wasn't it?' he whispered.

'Bargus,' said Bartlett, 'that was the dumbest excuse I've ever heard.'

Bargus shrugged. 'Sometimes dumb things are the cleverest.'

Bartlett nudged him to get moving. They went around the corner and followed the passage. They went deeper into the building. There were fewer windows, less light. Suddenly Bargus stopped.

'I think this is it.'

'You *think?*'

'I've never actually been to the throne room before. I'm a new guard, Bartlett, don't forget.'

Bargus hesitated. He obviously wanted someone else to open the door. But what if it wasn't the throne room? What if it was the kitchen, or the billiards room, or the Pasha's bedroom? At least a guard might have an excuse for poking around, even if he was only looking for the turban that was on top of his head!

'Hurry up, Bargus,' hissed Bartlett.

Bargus put his fingers on the door handle. Slowly, he turned it.

The door opened with a groan. Bargus looked inside. A moment later he disappeared. Bartlett and Jacques followed him in.

It was the throne room. Bartlett and Jacques recognised it at once. Moonlight streamed in through the tall windows. But where was Bargus?

'Is that it?'

They jumped with fright. Bargus laughed. He was sitting on the Pasha's throne.

'Well,' said Bargus, pointing towards the back of the room, 'is that it?'

Bartlett nodded.

'I still don't see why you need to take it like this,' said Bargus. 'If you need it to get the Pasha's son, I'm sure the

Pasha would give it to you.'

'Well, to be honest, we don't *need* to take it like this—'

'Why didn't you tell me that before?' cried Bargus loudly, forgetting where he was. 'Why did you make me bring you here?' He jumped off the throne and ran to Bartlett. 'I've risked everything!' he hissed, 'and all along you could have just gone to the Pasha and asked for it.'

Bartlett didn't reply. Gozo had said that the Pasha wanted to send his soldiers to destroy the Underground. Even if the Pasha gave them the mirror, he would send his men to follow them. And Bartlett was *not* going to allow an army to go tearing into the Underground, attacking Prule, and Avner, and the Ahsap.

'Bartlett! Why?'

'We didn't want to ask the Pasha.'

'You didn't *want* to? Well, I didn't *want* to be a guard for six years, and march around the stonefields, and talk to More all day. We can't all do what we want. I think I'll just go and let the Pasha know exactly what you're up to.'

Bartlett shook his head. 'It's too late for that, Bargus.'

'Too late? It's never too late! Just try and stop me— you and Jacques both.'

Jacques shrugged. He walked towards the back of the room.

'Go and tell the Pasha,' said Bartlett. 'But you'd better be ready to explain how we got here.' Bartlett paused, watching the look change on Bargus' face. 'You're with us now, Bargus. None of us is safe until we're *all* out of here.'

'You tricked me!'

Bartlett shook his head. 'You'll understand later. You might even thank me.'

Bargus snorted. Bartlett turned away. There were more important things to do, they couldn't stand around talking in the throne room forever.

Jacques was far away at the end of the room. There on the wall, hung the mirror: the Pasha's mirror that was said to reflect all objects without the slightest imperfection.

The mirror held the image of the room: the dark shapes of the thrones, the bright stripes of moonlight across the floor. And high in one corner, framed by a window, as clear and crisp as if it had risen along the surface of the mirror itself . . . the moon, shining pale and cool.

Bartlett joined Jacques at the end of the room. As Bargus watched, they took the mirror off the wall and carried it away.

Whether the Pasha's mirror did give the most perfect reflection of any mirror in the world, as people said, Bartlett and Jacques le Grand could not tell. But if someone had told them it was the biggest, longest, heaviest mirror in the world, they would both have agreed. Soon their arms were aching, their wrists felt ready to snap. They twisted their backs to get it around corners, they grimaced with effort. And all the time they moved as carefully as they could, breathed quietly, whispered instructions to each other and then paused to see if anyone had heard. Bargus went ahead to check that no one was coming.

They brought the mirror out into the courtyard. Each footstep was like an explosion, so loud did it seem to them in the surrounding silence. Bargus was already at the door on the other side of the courtyard. He beckoned to them to hurry. The sweat was pouring off their faces. They ran with the mirror and didn't stop until they had got it through the doorway and Bargus had shut the door behind them.

Now they faced the stairs and passages of the secret exit from the palace. There was still danger here, since another guard might meet them on the way out. The stairs were steep, the corners sharp, and they slowed down more often than they speeded up. Again and again Bargus ran ahead to see whether the way was clear. One tunnel, two tunnels; two sets of stairs, three sets, Bargus racing ahead, Bargus coming back. Soon they would be out into the alley and safe. A fourth set of stairs, a fifth

room, and here was Bargus again, coming back, coming
back fast . . .

'Hide! Hide!'

Hide where? Bartlett and
Jacques looked around.
They were in a corridor.
A bare corridor.

'Go back!'

'Go back where?'

'Guards, Bartlett.
Guards. Ahead.
Coming this way.'

There was nowhere
to go. Bartlett stared at
Jacques. Jacques put
down his end of the
mirror and pointed,
with one finger, at the
wall of the corridor.

Bartlett nodded.
There was no time for more
than that.

'What are you doing?' demanded Bargus.

They flipped the mirror. Its wooden back faced
outwards. They leaned it against the wall. Then they
crawled into the gap, as far in as they could, so that
no one could see them unless they crawled in after
them.

'Hide, I said. You call this hiding?'

'Lead them away from it, Bargus. They won't know it's a mirror.'

'Of course they'll know it's a mirror. What else will they think it is? A tabletop? Come out of there! Come—'

'Bargus. Is that you?'

'Pargon. Fancy meeting you here!'

'Going out, Bargus?'

Bartlett and Jacques could hear Pargon scuffling and staggering along. Others followed. There were voices. Drunken guards shouting *'Bargus!'* as they recognised him. Then there was a thud.

'My knee! Oh, my knee!'

'Who left this tabletop here?'

'It's the carpenters, they're always leaving things around.'

'They left a cupboard once and I locked myself inside.'

'How could you lock yourself inside?'

'I'll bet his mother locked him in!'

 'Come on, let's get rid of this tabletop, boys.'

'No! No, we shouldn't.'

'Why not?'

'Because . . . because . . . Wait! Does anyone know where my turban is?'

'Bargus, it's on top of your head!'

'On your head, Bargus!'

'Whose head?'

'His head, not your head!'

'Come on, boys, I think Bargus needs a drink. Do you need a drink, Bargus?'

'Well, I suppose I could . . .'

'Drink, Bargus. Come on!'

'Come on! . . . Come on! . . .Come on! . . .'

The 'Come ons' disappeared into the distance, together with the sound of footsteps.

Then there was silence.

Bartlett and Jacques crept out. The corridor was empty. There was no sign of Bargus. They lifted the mirror and set off.

In an alley not far from the Pasha's palace, a doorway opened. A stringly figure came out, looked around, and waved twice.

Further down the street, there was a wagon standing by the wall. In the shadows, the driver stirred. The wagon began to move. It came to a halt in front of the doorway.

The figure had gone back inside. Now he came out again with a second person, and between them they were carrying something long, heavy and flat. It might have been a tabletop, although it would have been large enough for twenty diners. They raised it onto the back of the wagon, sliding it on with care. Then they jumped up after it.

The wagon moved off.

'Take your time,' murmured Bartlett from the back of the wagon. 'No need to tire the horses. Just get us past the city gate. They'll never work out who it was.'

'All right,' said More, and he gave the reins a gentle flick.

Chapter 23

At nine o'clock the next morning, the door to the Pasha's throne room opened. A man went in with a broom and a pan. He began to sweep the floor.

It was the day of the merchants' medal ceremony. At the start of his reign, the Pasha had not given medals to the merchants, and they had begun to feel that nobody really appreciated them. The Pasha was always giving awards to his soldiers, for example, and praising his officials, and even occasionally thanking teachers in public! But what about the merchants? Who brought the fabulous silks that the Pasha liked to wear? Who brought the clocks that the Pashanne liked to hang on her walls? Who brought the coloured glass jugs, for that matter, that everyone thought were so wonderful? Merchants, that was who! Of course, they didn't do it for free, and in fact the price of these things always seemed to rise once the Pasha or Pashanne was interested in them. But teachers didn't teach for free either, said the merchants to one another, and they said it so often, and so loudly, and so unhappily, each time they passed each other in the bazaar, and each time they met in one of the coffee houses in the square, and each time they gathered for a banquet in one of their big houses, that the Pasha eventually decided that he had to do *something* to keep them quiet. So once a year the Pasha gave them medals.

Medals for what? Medals for . . . making life silky, or clockety, or glassy, medals with inscriptions like 'Silver Medal for Services of Silkification', which, to tell the truth, were just a little bit absurd. Yet the merchants smiled proudly, and bowed graciously, thinking that their work had been recognised.

The sweeper noticed at once that the Pasha's mirror was missing. 'Good,' he thought to himself, 'they've finally decided to take it down and give it a new frame!' Everyone knew that the Pashanne thought the frame was too old-fashioned and had even picked out a new one for it, and the sweeper was inclined to agree with her.

At ten o'clock, two guards turned up to take their places on either side of the thrones. 'They've taken the mirror for its new frame,' called out the sweeper, who was just leaving. The guards frowned. To tell the truth, they spent most of their time during these boring cere-monies staring at the mirror, admiring their splendid orange uniforms and the shimmering feathers in their turbans. It was going to be a long morning!

At ten-thirty the merchants began to arrive. They all looked to see the Pasha's famous mirror. It wasn't there. One or two of them began to grumble. 'He wouldn't have taken it down if it was the *teachers* today!' said the grumblers, and others nodded, because deep down some of the merchants didn't really feel that the Pasha took their medals seriously, and some of the inscriptions had become *so* absurd, like 'Bronze Medal for Bringing

Bronze Plates' that they were almost worse than having no medals at all.

At ten to eleven the Conductor of Ceremonies arrived, followed by a boy who carried the medals on a big velvet cushion. The Conductor had a long scroll under his arm with all the names of the merchants who were going to receive medals and the reasons for their awards. He had worked past midnight to think of reasons and in the end had run out of ideas. He had to copy some of them from the year before. Luckily, he always kept the scrolls.

The Conductor saw that the mirror was missing. He crossed his arms in annoyance. How could he conduct the ceremony without the mirror? Well, of course, he *could* conduct the ceremony without the mirror, because the mirror had nothing at all to do with it in *practice*, but in *principle* it was he who should have decided whether it was needed. Why hadn't he been told that it would be missing? The Pashanne! He bet the Pashanne was behind it. She was always telling the Pasha to do things behind his back.

At eleven o'clock the Pasha and Pashanne arrived. The room fell silent. Even the grumblers stopped talking.

The Pashanne noticed. Good, she thought, it's finally getting the new frame. The Pasha was probably keeping it as a surprise for her. How sweet! She turned and smiled at the Pasha. The Pasha smiled back, without any idea what he was smiling about.

The Conductor of Ceremonies noticed the smile with anger. What further proof did he need? 'Pasha, shall we start?' he said abruptly.

The Pasha had hardly sat down. The merchants were bowing. Merchants always bowed longer and lower than anybody else, and the Pasha would happily have let them bow for another hour. If he had to give them these ridiculous medals, it was the least they could do.

'All right,' the Pasha muttered. Another long ceremony was about to begin. 'And do it quickly this time. Last year it took you all day.'

'Pasha, it did not take all day,' said the Conductor, who was still feeling irritated about the mirror. 'It took two hours, not counting your speech. What am I supposed to do if you never let me know *anything* in advance?'

The Pasha frowned. What did that have to do with it? The Conductor had never before asked to know about the speech in advance. Anyway, it was always the same speech every year. 'Well, count it, count it, then!' the Pasha said. 'He should count the speech if he wants to, shouldn't he?'

159

The Pashanne didn't reply. She was still smiling. Someone seemed to have made her very happy. The Pasha hoped it was him.

The Conductor put a hand on his head to make sure his long brown wig was sitting straight. 'Honoured merchants,' he said in his deepest and most dignified voice: 'the Pasha!'

The Pasha stood up. He knew the speech by heart. *Merchants*, it began, *I welcome you to my palace*. At this point he would always spread his arms, and gaze right across the audience, from one side to the other, as if to show that he was taking them into both his heart and his home.

'Merchants, I welcome you to my palace.'

The Pasha spread his arms. He turned his head to one side of the room and slowly began to gaze across his audience, with a warm, welcoming expression on his face, not forgetting, of course, to glance up for just an instant to see his fine, welcoming figure reflected in the . . .

The Pasha's face froze. The warm, welcoming expression turned to stone.

A moment later, he appeared to stumble, and would have fallen to the floor if not for one of the guards, who sprang forward to catch him.

'Get them out,' hissed the Pasha.

'Who?' whispered the Conductor in alarm.

'The merchants, that's who. Get them out! Get them out!'

'Why?'

'Because the mirror's gone,' said the Pashanne, who understood everything immediately. 'Someone's taken the mirror, haven't they dear?'

'Of course someone's taken the mirror!' said the Pasha. 'Where else is it?'

'I thought you'd ordered it to be taken,' said the Conductor. He couldn't help feeling relieved. The Pasha hadn't ordered the mirror to be removed after all! Of course, now they had another problem, but it seemed much less of a problem to the Conductor than the idea of the Pasha deciding things without him.

The merchants were watching, puzzled. What was going on up there in front of the thrones? Everyone was huddled around the Pasha. Was he ill?

'You can't send them out,' whispered the Pashanne. 'They won't be happy. They'll talk. Give your speech. And you,' she added, turning to the Conductor, 'finish it quickly.'

The Pasha and the Conductor nodded. The Pashanne went back to her throne. The guards moved away. The Pasha gave his speech. It started just like the one he gave each year but it ended a bit more quickly. 'Merchants,' he said, 'welcome to my palace. Come and get your medals.' He sat back in his chair with a wave of the hand. The Conductor called out the names as if it were some kind of race. He didn't bother with the reasons.

Not even his specially designed uniform and fine wig were enough to hide the fact that the proceedings had very little dignity, almost no dignity at all. The merchants were falling over each other to get to the Pasha before the next one pushed them over. It was finished in twenty minutes. Five minutes later, the merchants were gone.

The Pasha clenched his fists. All of the rage that he had bottled up inside him exploded. He jumped up. 'Where is my mirror?' he shouted, his face red with anger. 'Who's taken it? I'll have them strung up in the sun and left to die of thirst with a bucket of water in front of them.'

'It's them!' The Pasha paced up and down. He could barely take his eyes off the bare wall where the mirror had hung.

'We can't be certain,' said the Conductor.

'Who else could it be? Who else would dare?'

The Conductor didn't answer. The Pashanne nodded. 'I agree. It must be them.'

'Hah!' cried the Pasha, glaring triumphantly. It was not often that the Pashanne agreed with him, and it reminded him of his good sense whenever it happened.

'They've come to mock me. They've come to take the mirror out of my very own palace. *You!*' he shouted, turning on his two guards, 'why didn't you stop them?'

The two guards glanced at each other in confusion. How were they supposed to stop people running off with mirrors when the Pasha expected them to be at his side night and day?

'It's not their fault, dear,' said the Pashanne, 'you can't blame them.'

'Who, then? Who can I blame?' demanded the Pasha, who wanted to blame somebody. In fact, the more he thought about it, the more he wanted to find someone to punish. Someone to string up in the hot sun, with a bucket of water just out of reach . . .

The Pashanne sat down. She was thinking. 'Perhaps they took it for a reason,' she said.

The Pasha laughed. 'Yes. I know a reason: to make a fool of me! They can't have Darian, they can't have their maps, so they thought—let's get something else. Oh, I should have got rid of them when I had the chance. I should have got two strong ropes—'

'Why couldn't they have the maps?' said the Pashanne.

'What?'

'Well, if they managed to get the mirror, surely they could have got the maps just as easily. They're only next door. But they took the mirror. Don't you think that means something?'

'Yes, it means they've made a fool of me! *You!*' he said

163

to the guards, 'get after them as fast as you can. Take as many men as you need. Take ten. Take twenty!'

'But . . . where . . . ?' stammered one of the guards.

'Where? To the stonefields. Where do you think? That's where they come from, those cavemen!'

The guards glanced at each other in dread. A trip to the stonefields? Bitter cold nights with only the hard ground for a bed, scorching days fit to fry an egg on your head? They shuddered. They hadn't spent years and years working themselves up through the ranks, getting into the Palace Guard, becoming one of the trusted few who served as the personal guards of the Pasha, in order to go off to the stonefields again.

'But who'll—'

'What? Who'll *what*?'

'Who'll look after you, Pasha?' said the guard.

'There are others, aren't there?'

'Then they should go.'

'Why should they go?'

'Because then we'll be able to stay to look after you,' said the guard.

'I caught you when you fell. Just now. Remember?' said the other.

'And I . . . would have caught you if he hadn't,' said the first. 'Now's the most dangerous time when you need your most trusted men, Pasha, now your . . . mirror's gone.'

The Pashanne rolled her eyes. 'All right. Go and find another.'

'Who, Pashanne?'

'Anyone. Bring back the first one you find.'

'Yes, Pashanne, yes,' said one of the guards, hurrying out of the throne room.

'Very wise. Very wise, Pashanne,' said the other, grinning enthusiastically.

They waited. It wasn't long before the door swung open again. The first guard came in dragging another one by the ear. He pushed him in front of the Pasha.

'Straighten up,' said the Pasha. 'You're new here, aren't you? Put your turban on properly.' The Pasha frowned. 'What's wrong with you?'

'Nuh . . . Nothing, Pasha.'

'You don't seem very pleased to be here.'

'I am pleased, Pasha.'

The Pasha wasn't convinced. 'What do you think?' he whispered to the Pashanne, 'he doesn't *really* look pleased, does he?'

'He's pleased enough,' said the Pashanne impatiently.

'Well,' said the Pasha, 'you should be pleased. What's your name?'

'Barg . . . Bargus, Pasha!'

'Bargbargus? That's a very odd name. One Barg is enough, don't you think? Now stop trembling. Why are you trembling? Listen to me, Bargbargus, we don't want tremblers in the Guard. If you can't stop trembling I'll have to throw you out.'

Bargus tried to stop trembling. But it was difficult. He was sure the Pasha had found out. Why else had he sent another guard to get him, cursing and shouting, dragging him along by the ear? Only the Pasha's mercy could save him now. What should he do? Fall on his knees? Confess everything?

'Listen, Bargbargus, someone has taken my mirror.'

Bargus froze. His blood had turned to ice. He could actually feel it crunching in his veins.

'I want it back.'

'Pasha, Pasha—'

'Take as many men as you need. Go to the stonefields. Look for two men: one lean and stringly, the other tall and broad. They call themselves Bartlett and Jacques le—' The Pasha stopped, frowning. 'Bargbargus, why are you on your knees? Did I ask you to kneel?'

'No,' muttered Bargus, almost faint with relief. The Pasha didn't know—at least, he didn't know about *him*.

'Then get up. It's an honour to serve your Pasha, but this . . . kneeling is ridiculous! Now, go, Bargbargus. And listen to me well . . .' The Pasha's voice was low and urgent. 'Bring me my mirror, and bring me the two men who took it. Bring them alive. Do you understand? I must have them alive.' The Pasha leaned forward. Everyone else leaned forward as well. 'How did they get the mirror? How did they pass through my palace? Did someone help them? This I must find out before they die. Bring them to me alive, Bargbargus!' The Pasha prodded his finger hard into Bargus' chest. 'Do not fail, or you yourself will suffer their fate.'

Bargus nodded. He took a step back. Everything was dark. His head was swimming.

The other guard pulled on his arm. Somehow he found himself outside the throne room once more.

'Go into the city and pick ten guardsmen to go with you,' said the guard. 'Be back in an hour. Your horses will be ready.'

Chapter 24

'You know, I never really believed in the Underground,' said More, 'not in all the time I patrolled the stonefields. When you told me you'd actually found it, you could have knocked me over with a chinip.'

Bartlett laughed. He was sitting on the front of the wagon with More. Jacques le Grand was resting in the back, keeping an eye on the mirror. More was meant to have left them with the wagon once they had passed the city gate. But he had stayed, not uttering a word of explanation, holding the reins and driving towards the stonefields.

It was already late in the afternoon. Soon they would have to find food and water for the horses. It had been a peaceful day. By the time the sun had risen, the City of Sun was far behind them. The sky was clear and a gentle breeze had kept them cool. There was plenty of food and wine in the wagon, packed by Sol. It was almost like a summer outing. The horses walked at a patient pace, neither fast nor slow, and the wheels of the wagon turned steadily.

'Is that why you decided to come with us?' said Bartlett.

'I suppose so,' said More. 'I wanted to see it.' More paused, frowning. Then he shrugged. 'Actually, I don't know, Bartlett. I didn't mean to come. But something stopped me getting off the wagon. I don't know what.'

Bartlett laughed. More started laughing as well. In the back, Jacques grinned.

'It's funny, isn't it?' said More.

'It *is* funny,' said Bartlett. 'I probably would have done the same myself.'

'True,' said More, 'but you wouldn't have spent six years wandering around the stonefields, looking for something you didn't even believe in.'

'No. I don't think I would have done that.'

'Why did I do it, Bartlett? All those years. Why?'

Bartlett shook his head. He didn't know. He didn't know why people got stuck doing things they disliked. But people did. More wasn't the only one.

The horses plodded on. The wagon trundled slowly behind them.

Later, they saw an inn in the distance. There was a stable behind it and a well in front. The sun was setting by the time they arrived. The Pasha's mirror, lying flat in the wagon, reflected the last rays of light.

They climbed down. More was about to go into the stable to see if there was hay for the horses. Bartlett and Jacques starting undoing the harnesses. They heard the sound of galloping coming towards them.

More turned and peered into the evening shadows. The sound grew louder. 'Someone else will be wanting to use the stable,' he said, still gazing into the dusk. 'I hope there's room for—'

More's voice stopped.

'How many are there, More?' asked Bartlett, working at one of the fastenings.

More didn't reply. Bartlett and Jacques looked up.

The galloping was close now.

'Bargus . . .' said More in astonishment.

Bargus jumped down. He was breathing heavily, as if he, and not his horse, had been galloping.

'What are you doing here, More?' he demanded.

'What are *you* doing here?' More replied in amazement.

'What am I doing here?' he cried bitterly. He tore the harness out of Bartlett's hands and began refastening it. 'Come on. Get moving. You can't stay here.'

'What's happened?' said Bartlett.

'Nothing! Everything! Bartlett, the day I met you was the worst day of my life.'

'I thought it was the best day of your life,' said More.

Bargus glared at him fiercely.

'I told you, Bargus, we didn't have to capture them.

We could have just gone back down that hill as if we'd seen nothing. But no, you *had* to be a hero. You *had*—'

'Come on,' Bargus snarled. 'Move. I've told you. There's no time.'

'The horses need water,' said Bartlett. He looked at Bargus' horse. Its flanks were heaving, its nostrils flared, still searching for air. 'Yours does too.'

'Well, come on, then, let's do it quickly. Quickly, Bartlett. You don't understand.'

'Then tell us.'

Bargus told them while the horses drank. He told them about the Pasha, and his orders. He told them about the ten men that he had taken, and how he led them towards the lakes, telling them that was where they had to go, and how he had managed to slip away while they sat down for lunch, and how he cut back across country by himself. Where the others were now, he had no idea: perhaps still heading for the lakes, perhaps returning to the city. How long it would be before they sent out another troop, he couldn't tell. Tomorrow perhaps, or tonight. There was little time. Wagons travelled slowly, horsemen fast. They couldn't rest. They had to keep going.

'So you came to help us,' said More. 'Bargus, that was very nice of you.'

'Oh, yes, very nice. What choice do I have? If I go back to the Pasha without these two—the Pasha punishes me. If I go back *with* them, they tell him how they got the mirror—and the Pasha still punishes me.'

'That's what happens when you make things up, Bargus. If only you'd told the truth about how we met them in the first place, none of this would have happened.'

'*More!*' cried Bargus. He tore his turban off his head and threw it on the ground in rage. 'Did you want to patrol the stonefields forever? Is that what you wanted?'

More scratched his chin. 'Not really.'

Bargus turned to Bartlett. 'You tricked me,' he said, 'you tricked me all along.'

Bartlett shook his head. No, he hadn't tricked him—it was Bargus who had tricked himself. But that didn't matter now. They both understood the situation.

'There's only one way out for me, isn't there?' said Bargus.

Bartlett nodded. 'If we get Darian back, the Pasha will forgive everything—the mirror, the lies, the sneaking off from your men, everything . . . perhaps.'

Bargus glanced at Jacques. Jacques was watching him closely.

'Let's go!' cried Bargus suddenly. 'Let's go! Let's get that boy.'

They travelled fast. They needed the wagon to carry the mirror, but never had a wagon moved so quickly. Day and night they travelled: two slept, two stayed awake. They didn't rest the horses, but changed them

whenever they came to an inn or stable—Bargus had
been given an order from the Pasha requiring anyone at
all to provide them with fresh horses. It was
supposed to be used to help catch Bartlett
and Jacques le Grand—now it was
helping them to escape. It was
enough to wave the paper in
the face of an innkeeper to
drive him to action.

It was a race, a race
to the stonefields.
Against whom?
They didn't know
if anyone was
pursuing
them.

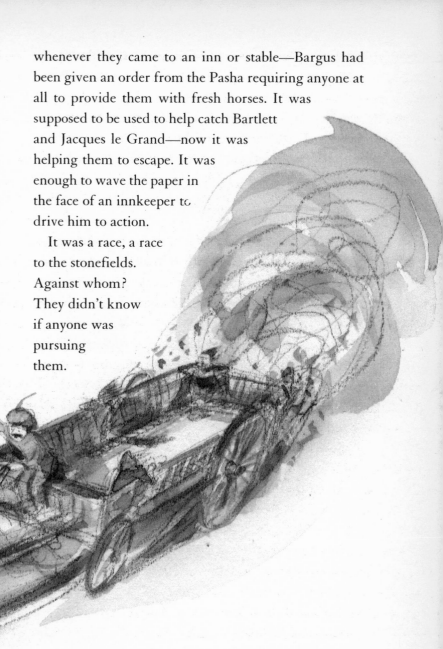

Uncertainty was more difficult than knowledge. They had a head start but they had no idea if it was enough.

Desperation seized the wagon, ruled it like an angry prince, ever waking, ever present. In their imagination they could feel the guards behind their backs, hear the thundering of their horses' hooves, feel their hot breath on their necks. Their own horses drove across the plain, pounding into the road, raising a cloud of dust that travelled with them like a swirling, choking cloak. But dust could not hide them from the pursuers in their minds. Faster, faster they drove, Bargus the fiercest of all, whipping the reins, shouting at the horses, wearing them out. The wagon creaked, groaned, its wheels spinning. It was never enough. When the wind rose he stood and raised his arms and cried out to the horses: 'Faster! Faster! You are slow, the wind is passing us.' And the horses, foam at the mouth, blood in their eyes, with the sound of Bargus' mad voice in their ears, galloped as if possessed by that same madness, if it is possible for a horse to be mad.

For two days, three nights, they travelled. And on the third day, with their last set of horses on the point of collapse, the red rock of the stonefields lay before them.

They left the wagon behind and carried the mirror onto the stone.

They went over the crest of a hill, dropped into a valley. Now the rust-red rock surrounded them. The valley was speckled with pillars. Suddenly it all came back to More and Bargus, the long, cold nights, the scorching days, the silence, the awful feeling of being cut off from everybody else.

'We're safe now,' said Bartlett.

'Safe?' said Bargus.

'They're watching us already.'

More and Bargus looked around. Their eyes narrowed in apprehension.

'It won't be long now,' said Bartlett.

'What?' whispered More.

Bartlett didn't reply. He and Jacques led the way, taking the front of the mirror, while More and Bargus came behind, glancing nervously over their shoulders.

Then one of the stone columns seemed to shimmer, or move, and in the blink of an eye there was a pale figure in a round goat's-hair hat standing beside it.

Chapter 25

'What's this?' said Avner, standing over the mirror. He made a face, baring his teeth and scrunching up his nose. He laughed. 'It's much better than polished rock,' he said.

Bartlett laughed. 'By the way, I should introduce you: More and Bargus.'

'Oh, I know them already.'

More and Bargus stared. They had been staring since the moment Avner appeared. He was Pale as the Moon.

'I've seen them lots of times. You used to wander around here with your spears, didn't you? You—you were dressed differently then,' Avner said to Bargus. 'Not so fine.'

'I'm . . . a Palace Guard now,' muttered Bargus.

'Is that good? It must be good, if you've got such bright clothes. What about you?' he said, turning to More.

'No, I'm not a Palace Guard,' More confessed.

'What happened? You always used to be together.'

More shrugged. Bargus looked away, biting his lip.

'Anyway,' said Avner, 'what are they doing here? It was just meant to be you and Jacques, Bartlett.'

'No it wasn't.'

'Of course it was. The Ahsap said: just you and Jacques. He said it four times at least!'

'Avner, stop exaggerating. He didn't say anything at all about other people coming with us. They gave us a lot of help. We couldn't have done it without them.'

'The Ahsap won't be happy. He'll capture them and never let them go. You know the rules, Bartlett.'

More and Bargus gazed at Bartlett with fear. Bartlett shook his head. 'The rules are changing, Avner.'

Avner led them deeper into the stonefields. They would have to send someone back later to give water and hay to the horses. Avner said he would arrange it, but they didn't have any hay. He hoped horses ate chinips.

The sun rose high. The heat was growing. The mirror seemed to get heavier and heavier, even with four people to carry it.

'Why don't we leave it behind?' said Avner when they stopped for a rest. 'It'll be much easier, and you can always come back for it later.'

'Avner,' said Bartlett, wiping the sweat from his brow, 'what are you talking about? The mirror's the whole point.'

'No, Bartlett. You were meant to bring the sun, remember?' Avner pointed at the sky. 'There it is. It hasn't moved.'

'Listen, Avner. When we take the mirror and put—' Bartlett stopped. He smiled and glanced at Jacques. Why explain? Avner had a big surprise in store.

Avner was waiting.

'Let's just keep the mirror, if you don't mind.'

'*I* don't mind,' said Avner. 'But *they* don't look very happy.'

And it was true, More and Bargus didn't look very happy, not because of the weight of the mirror—although that wasn't helping—but because of their fear of what would happen to them once they arrived at the Underground. Bargus might well have turned around and gone back, if not for the fact that there was nothing waiting for him at home but the Pasha's anger, which only the return of Darian would soothe. And More . . . More stayed for reasons that he could not easily explain, as he had stayed on the wagon when he drove it through the city gate, because something *made* him stay, perhaps the fact that he had spent so many years here, on these stonefields, imagining a place and a people that he had never actually seen—and the time had come to face them.

Yet as Avner lead them on, chattering, asking questions and demanding replies—no matter how friendly he became and how readily Bartlett talked with him, or how often Jacques grinned at something he said—More and Bargus couldn't help looking over their shoulders, glancing nervously up at the hills and around the columns, as if they were still guardsmen patrolling the stonefields and the Undergrounders, out here in this wilderness of rock, were still their enemies.

That night they slept beneath the icy sky. When they awoke, Avner was gone. He had crept off to sleep in the

Underground, but he was back just after dawn, bub-
bling with excitement.

'Everyone knows you're coming!' he said.

'Really?' said Bargus uneasily. 'How long will it take
us to get there?'

'Only a few hours. Don't worry, everyone will be
waiting!'

Bartlett and Jacques saw it in the distance: the broad
pillar that marked the entrance to the Underground.

They marched towards it. More and Bargus didn't
realise what it was. When they arrived, Avner disappeared around the other side of the pillar. An instant
later, the column shimmered, moved, and was still
again.

The entrance to the Underground was in front of
them.

More and Bargus stared at the red rock steps that led
into the ground. They blinked, as if they thought they
were dreaming. How often, in all the years they had
patrolled the stonefields, had they camped in this valley?
How many times might they have walked past this very
place?

'Where's the Ahsap now, Avner?' asked Bartlett.

'In the counsel chamber. I told him I would bring you
there.'

'Good. Now listen, Avner. You go to the counsel
chamber. We're staying here.'

'But—'

'You'll understand later. Now, go to the counsel chamber, run as fast as you can.'

'And what will I do when I get there? What will I say? He's expecting you.'

'No, he's expecting the sun.' Bartlett grinned. 'Say nothing. Just open the door . . . and stand back.'

Avner didn't understand. 'Just open the door? Open the door and stand back? That's all?'

Bartlett nodded. He glanced up at the sky. The sun was near its zenith. 'Run, Avner!' There was no time to explain more. 'Run as fast as you can. And if there are people in the passage, tell them to stand back. Tell them to get out of the way. It's important.'

'All right. I'll do it!'

Avner raced down the steps. They heard him running down the passage. Then the echo of his footsteps faded away.

More and Bargus were staring at the opening into which he had disappeared.

Bartlett looked up at the sky again. 'How long do we have, Jacques. About fifteen minutes?'

Jacques glanced up. He nodded.

180

Chapter 26

The mirror was wide, the walls of the steps were solid rock. They took the mirror down slowly. Jacques carried the weight at the bottom, coming down the steps backwards, with Bartlett below to guide him. More and Bargus lifted at the top. The mirror scraped the walls as they went down. Where the rough rock of the wall stuck out, they had to tilt the mirror to avoid it, and the muscles in Jacques' arms bulged, his face went red with the strain.

Finally Jacques reached the bottom. Now came the moment of suspense, the part in the plan of which not even Bartlett could be sure: the mirror had to rest face up on the steps, perfectly evenly. If it was tilted even a fraction to one side to fit in, the plan wouldn't work. Jacques lowered the end of the mirror slowly. There was barely a centimetre to spare. It crunched. Bartlett winced. When he looked again, the mirror was lying evenly on the steps.

Ahead, he knew, Avner was running. Ten minutes must have passed. Soon Avner would reach the Ahsap's door. The sun was nearing its zenith.

The mirror was flooding sunlight into the passage. The flames of the lamps had disappeared, had become invisible against it. But the sunlight was hitting the roof. An intense beam of white light ran along the ceiling.

Further down the passage, there would still be darkness, the flames of the lamps would still be flickering against the walls.

'What's happening?' called Bargus.

'We have to change the angle,' said Bartlett to Jacques. Jacques nodded. 'Angle it!' Bartlett cried up the steps.

'Which way?'

Jacques pointed to the roof.

'Up!' cried Bartlett.

'Our end?' called Bargus.

Jacques nodded.

More and Bargus lifted. The sunlight jumped. Now it was on the floor.

'Less.'

The beam darted back to the roof.

182

'More.'

'What?'

'No, lift it more! More!'

The mirror crunched against the wall. The sunlight darted around unsteadily, bouncing over the sides of the passage and ending up along one corner of the floor.

'Is that all right?'

'No!' cried Bartlett. 'Listen, first of all, get it in the middle. Keep it even. You've got the mirror tilted to one side.'

'It's More! He's not lifting enough.'

'It's Bargus. He's lifting too much.'

Jacques raised an eyebrow.

'Quiet!' cried Bartlett. Time was running out. Avner must be almost at the Ahsap's door. The sun must be at its peak. 'Bargus, drop your side just a bit. Just a fraction. Carefully.'

The sunlight moved out onto the floor.

'A bit more . . . a bit more . . . That's it! Stop!'

The light was now in the very middle of the floor. It ran along the rock.

'Now . . . bring it down. Together . . . Steady . . . Steady . . .'

The beam moved. It stretched further along the floor. Further and further. Now Bartlett and Jacques couldn't see where it ended. Their own shadows seemed to stretch forever.

'A bit more. Perfect . . . Careful . . . Steady . . . Steady . . . *Stop!*'

The beam lifted off the floor. Bartlett and Jacques ducked. The rays of the sun, bouncing off the mirror, flew over their heads. Instantaneously, too fast for the eye to see, the rays of light tore along the passage, past flame after flame, tunnel after tunnel.

And the passage was perfectly straight. There was nothing to stop the sunlight but the door at the end.

Avner had run all the way, pounding, shouting 'Get back! Get back into the tunnels!' to all the people who had come to see Bartlett and Jacques return. He was panting for air. For the last few desperate steps he kept himself going by keeping his eye on the flame above the door of the counsel chamber, as if that alone could draw him on. Now the door itself was before him. He could almost grasp the handle. *'Open the door and stand back. Open the door and stand back,'* he was repeating wildly to himself. He grabbed the handle.

In the last split second before he opened it, before he could even understand what it meant, he noticed something strange. The flame above the door disappeared. Instead, he saw a shadow.

His own shadow—crisp, clear and black, its arm reaching out—loomed up on the door in front of him!

Avner turned the handle and stood back.

The Ahsap, sitting directly opposite the door on his throne, cried out.

The counsellors stared, dumbstruck, shielding their eyes. The Ahsap's face was bathed in a pure white light. The room was bright, as they had never seen it. The lamps on the walls, the starlit ceiling, were no longer visible. But the polished walls were dazzling red, the water in the pool flashed and sparkled.

The sun had come to the City of Flames.

Chapter 21

The sun had moved from its zenith, and the mirror had been left lying on the steps, so the sunlight was no longer aiming directly into the Ahsap's counsel chamber by the time Bartlett, Jacques, More and Bargus arrived. Yet enough sunlight was still reflected down the corridor by the Pasha's flawless mirror to make the flames of the lamps seem dim and puny, and to make the counsel chamber brighter than a thousand of these lamps could ever have done.

The Ahsap was waiting for them.

'You are a very clever man, Bartlett,' he said, after Bartlett explained to him about the mirror.

'Not clever. Inventive, perhaps.'

'Is there a difference?'

Bartlett shrugged. He would prefer to be called inventive than clever, even if there wasn't a difference.

'You brought the sun.' The Ahsap shook his head, smiling. 'I thought I had set you an impossible task. But you succeeded. And I believe I owe you something.'

Bartlett nodded. He looked at the counsellors on their benches. They were watching him with a mixture of admiration and dislike, impressed by the idea of the mirror, unhappy at giving Bartlett his reward. Only the youngest counsellor gazed at him thoughtfully, without a trace of ill will.

There was another door behind the counsellors' benches. Out came Prule, and with him, Darian.

Prule whispered in the boy's ear. Darian glanced at Bartlett in disbelief. He looked back at Prule once more, and the old man nodded. Hesitantly, Darian walked towards Bartlett.

'Prule says you're going to take me home,' said Darian.

Bartlett nodded.

'But they told me I would never leave.'

'They were wrong,' said Bartlett.

The boy looked at Bartlett for a moment longer, as if still not sure whether to believe him.

'Do you want to go?' asked Bartlett.

Suddenly there was no longer any doubt in the boy's face. 'Yes! Yes I do! Take me home. Please. My father will reward you.'

'He doesn't need to,' said Bartlett.

The boy frowned. 'No?' Suddenly he started smiling.

'You see,' said Bartlett, 'you just did.'

Bartlett glanced at Prule. There was a tear in the old man's eye. He wiped it away with a wisp of his beard.

'Well,' said the Ahsap, '*that's* settled. Now we only have one other problem—these two!'

He pointed at More and Bargus. They flinched, as if his finger were able to shoot arrows.

'I told them!' cried Avner, 'I told them, Ahsap. If they came with us they'd have to stay forever. Come on, Prule, let's take them to your room.'

Bartlett shook his head.

'I did, I did tell them, Ahsap! It's the rule, I told them. I know you think I'm exaggerating, but I definitely—'

'Quiet, Avner,' said the Ahsap.

'Yes, Ahsap. But I did . . . tell them,' he whispered.

Around him, the Ahsap could tell, his counsellors were growing restless. He could already hear them mumbling under their breath. Their legs were twitching and their arms itched. Soon they would be on their feet, shouting to get his attention. Yet he continued to gaze at Bartlett.

'The sun has come into your city, Ahsap.'

The Ahsap nodded.

'Let them go.'

The Ahsap examined More and Bargus. 'Are they going to come back?' he asked.

'Not if you don't invite them,' said Bartlett.

'Then they can go.'

'*Go?*' squeaked one of the counsellors. The others were too shocked to speak.

'And when you take them back, how will you explain this to the Pasha, Bartlett?' said the Ahsap. 'What will you tell him?'

'I will tell him . . . that the sun has come to the Underground,' Bartlett said gravely. 'That now you both share it.'

The Ahsap considered. He nodded. 'I have often wondered,' he said, as if thinking aloud, 'what would happen if we and the Overgrounders could . . . speak with one another.'

'I think that would be a very interesting thing to find out,' said Bartlett.

'Perhaps, since you have brought a couple of them to us, we should send one or two of our people to them.'

The Ahsap turned to the youngest counsellor.

'Not her?' . . . *'Again?'*

'Will you go?' asked the Ahsap, ignoring the shouts of the other counsellors.

The youngest counsellor nodded.

'Come here, then,' said the Ahsap. He took a small book out of his pocket. 'If Bartlett takes you, as he says, and if you are able to speak with the Pasha, give this to him, as a mark of my appreciation.'

'To the Pasha?'

'No, to Bartlett.' The Ahsap glanced at the explorer. 'I suspect I won't have the chance to thank him again myself.'

Bartlett nodded. Explorers rarely visit a place more than once, and this was already the second time that he and Jacques had come to the City of Flames.

The Ahsap still had a thoughtful look on his face. 'And perhaps . . . Avner as well,' he said eventually. 'He seems to get on very well with Overgrounders.'

'Yes, Ahsap! I get on very well, *very well*—'

'Avner! Not *too* well . . .'

'No, Ahsap. I was just . . . exaggerating . . . a little bit . . .'

'Good,' said Bartlett. He bowed.

The Ahsap smiled. 'Not so deep a bow, Bartlett. It is

an honour to have met such a clever—such an *inventive* man.'

They started leaving the chamber, first Avner, then Bargus and More, Jacques and the counsellor. Bartlett and Darian left last. Prule waved goodbye, wiping his eyes with a wisp of his beard.

A moment later the counsellors were in uproar, pushing, shoving, dancing and shouting. But Bartlett had already closed the door behind him and was walking away down the passage of rock, into the sunlight, past curious Undergrounders who had come out to see the strangers leave.

'You know,' Bartlett said to Darian, putting a hand on his shoulder, 'you remind me of someone.'

'Who?'

'Oh, you'll find out soon enough.'

Chapter 28

Gozo and Darian stared at each other. Their eyes popped and their mouths dropped open.

They were as alike as two cherries on a stalk— two cherries with eyes who couldn't believe what they were seeing.

But that only lasted an instant.

'Mr Bartlett!'

'Mama!'

They raced past each other. Darian almost leapt at the thrones. Gozo threw himself at the explorers. When he had finished hugging Bartlett, he jumped up and grabbed Jacques as well.

'Yes ... well ... I'm happy to see you as well, Gozo ...'
Jacques spluttered, gently prising Gozo's hands from
around his neck.

Bartlett laughed. Mirta, unable to restrain herself, had
rushed from the corner of the throne room and was hugging and kissing everybody, Darian, the Pashanne, and
even the Pasha himself.

'Yes ... Mirta ... it is a happy day, isn't it?' said the
Pasha, trying to set her gently aside. But even the Pasha
was too happy to get upset.

Gozo was so excited he started hugging Bartlett once
more, and it was only the look in Jacques' eyes, as he
turned to grab him again, that finally made him stop.

'Well, Bartlett,' said the Pasha, 'you brought him
back. We had given up hope. In fact, we thought you
stole our mirror!'

'We did steal your mirror.'

'Oh.' The Pasha frowned. 'I'm not sure I really
approve of that. I don't think we mentioned the mirror
when we spoke, did we? In fact—'

'If they took the mirror,' whispered the Pashanne,
'I'm sure they had a good reason for it.'

'Yes. Yes, of course.' The Pasha smiled. 'I don't suppose
we can have it back now?'

'No,' said Bartlett.

'No. Oh, well, never mind. Never mind,' the Pasha
said to himself, because, of course, he really did mind,
never having expected to lose his mirror, but when he
glanced at his wife, and saw the way she smiled and

192

nodded at him, he realised that he *shouldn't* mind, and he decided that he had better try not to.

The Pasha looked at the others standing with Bartlett. Suddenly he noticed Bargus. '*You!* Weren't you the Guard we sent to get our mirror back? What was your name again? Barg some- thing. Barg . . . Bargbargus! That's it! What happened, Bargbargus? You're a terrible mess. Look at your uniform! You took ten guardsmen and they all came back complaining you'd disappeared.'

'He helped us,' said Bartlett.

'I didn't tell him to help you. I told him to *catch* you! Bargbargus, I'm going to have you taken out and—'

The Pashanne's hand rested lightly on her husband's arm. 'He *helped* them, dear.'

'Of course he did. Of course. I was just saying that I was going to have him taken out and . . . and given an orchard, that's what!'

'An orchard?' said the Conductor of Ceremonies in alarm. The Pasha was always giving orchards away. Soon there would be none left to be given to him!

'Yes. And to the other one as well. What's his name?'

'More,' said More.

'*More?*' said the Pasha. 'What kind of names are they giving our soldiers nowadays? This really is ridiculous.'

The Pasha shook his head. 'All right, More and Bargbargus, an orchard each. Make a note!' he said to the Conductor.

'Wait until Sol finds out about this!' whispered More.

'And now—these two,' said the Pasha, pointing at Avner and the Ahsap's counsellor, 'I suppose they're from the Underground. They're pale enough!'

'Actually, they are. Pasha, the sun has come to the Underground,' said Bartlett gravely. 'They share it with you now.'

'So?' The Pasha glanced at his wife. 'I suppose I'm going to have to hang these two,' he whispered. 'What a shame. It's such a happy day, and now I'm going to have to spoil it with a hanging. Still, I suppose it can't be helped, and it's all for the best in the—'

'Why don't we see what they want?' said the Pashanne.

The Pasha frowned. See what they want? The Pashanne really did have such extraordinary ideas sometimes! Still, he didn't want to make her angry, especially with Darian, who had been away so long, sitting on her lap. And her extraordinary ideas *did* have a habit of turning out to be extraordinarily clever . . .

'All right,' said the Pasha loudly, 'we don't really like people from the Underground. What do you want?'

The counsellor stepped forward. 'Our Ahsap—'

'Your *what?*'

'Our Ahsap would like to see what would happen if we began talking to each other.'

'Talking? To each other?'

The counsellor nodded.

'And you might like these,' said Avner, taking a step forwards and holding up a big bunch of chinips.

'What are they?' said the Pasha, wrinkling his nose.

'Chinips,' said Darian, 'they're nice if you fry them.'

'Or you can eat them raw. If you eat three bunches of chinips a day you'll never go blind, deaf, dumb or dreary. And you'll never get old, either.'

'Avner!' said Bartlett.

'Well . . . I was exaggerating a bit. But they are good for you. And we've got fish as well.'

'Really?' said the Pasha. 'And what do you want for your chinips and fish?'

'Goats. And a mirror, if you have another one.'

The Pasha crossed his arms. He looked at the Pashanne, as if he didn't know what to make of it all.

'And our people?' said the Pashanne, 'what about them?'

'They're safe,' said the counsellor.

'When can we have them back?'

'When will you stop sending soldiers to search for us?'

'Oh, this is ridiculous!' whispered the Pasha to his wife. 'Stop sending soldiers? What else am I meant to do with them? They can't *all* guard me. Let's hang these two. Let's just hang—'

The Pasha stopped in mid-sentence. His eyes almost popped out of his head. It was Darian who had put his hand quickly on the Pasha's arm, and who said, in a tone which could have come from the Pashanne herself: 'If we hang them, I don't think we're going to get our people back.'

'No,' said the Ahsap's counsellor, 'but if you don't hang us, who knows what might happen next?'

The Pasha stared. He had no idea. He tried to imagine. All around the throne room, others tried to imagine as well. Even the guards looked as though they were thinking about it.

Suddenly there was a cough. It came from Jacques. It was a loud cough, and it made everyone look up. He nudged Bartlett.

'Yes,' said Bartlett, 'there is one other thing.'

'I know what you want,' said the Pashanne. She motioned to the Conductor of Ceremonies, who motioned to a guard, who stepped out of the room and came back with a bag.

'Please give it to Mr Bartlett,' said the Pashanne.

The guard held out the bag. Jacques took it. He opened the bag and began checking the scrolls.

'They're all there,' said the Pashanne. 'We didn't know what to do with them. What are they, anyway?'

'The Margoulis Caverns!' cried Gozo for the four hundredth time.

'That's right,' said Bartlett.

'Not the Underground?'

'I've never *been* to the Underground!' cried Gozo excitedly. 'Don't you believe me now?'

'Yes,' said the Pashanne.

'Finally!' Gozo shook his head in disbelief.

'Mr Bartlett, these people don't believe *anything* you say.'

Jacques closed the bag.

'Well, we'll be going,' said Bartlett.

'Already?' said Gozo. He looked suddenly at Mirta.

The old woman left Darian and came to Gozo. She smiled and touched his cheek. 'Perseverance,' said Mirta. 'I never knew a boy who persevered so much. I'm sure you'll be a great explorer.'

Gozo tried to smile.

'Goodbye, Gozo.'

'Goodbye, Mirta.'

Bargus and More were watching. 'Goodbye,' said Bartlett. He grinned. More grinned as well. Bargus eyed him stonily. 'I told you you'd thank me, Bargus,' Bartlett whispered.

Jacques and Gozo were already at the door. The counsellor came to Bartlett and handed him the Ahsap's book.

'The Ahsap would wish me to thank you. See: already we have begun to talk with one another.'

Bartlett nodded. Avner had handed out chinips to everyone, and was standing next to the Pasha, explaining which were the best parts to eat.

'How many goats did you say you wanted?' said the Pasha, munching on a leaf.

They walked through the city. News had spread. Once again, people fell silent and crowds divided. Now there was not hostility in their glances, but wonder and admiration.

'I knew you'd come back, Mr Bartlett. I always knew,' said Gozo.

'There were the maps as well,' said Jacques, just in case Gozo had forgotten.

But Gozo wasn't thinking about them. 'Was it a good adventure, Mr Bartlett? Was it *very* exciting?'

'Oh, about average,' said Bartlett.

'Better than going on the ice voyage for the melidrop?'

Bartlett glanced at Jacques. Jacques shrugged. 'About the same, I'd say.'

Suddenly Gozo jumped up and down. 'It isn't fair!' he cried excitedly. 'It just isn't fair! I always miss out on the best part. All the time you were out there, I was stuck in the palace eating marzipan and honey.'

'And pomegranates.'

'Exactly!'

'It *is* bad luck,' said Bartlett. 'But on the other hand, if you hadn't been stuck there, we wouldn't have had the adventure at all! I suppose we should thank you, shouldn't we, Jacques? *Jacques?*'

'Thank you,' mumbled Jacques.

Gozo frowned. Somehow being thanked didn't quite make up for it.

They turned a corner. The city gate lay ahead of them. From the crossroads beyond it, one road ran east to the stonefields, one north to the lakes, and another south towards the sea.

They stood at the crossroads.

'Do you remember, Jacques,' said Bartlett, 'how we always wanted to explore the Gircassian Rift, but we never had the time?'

Jacques nodded.

'Well, I suppose first we'll have to find a ship that will take Gozo home.'

Gozo's eyes went wide with dismay. His voice trembled with disappointment. 'Mr Bartlett, you're not going to go to that . . . rift without me?'

'You wouldn't be interested, Gozo. It's only the deepest, longest canyon in the world. Its floor is covered with dinosaur footprints . . .'

'And there are rock pools of coral in steaming hot springs,' added Jacques.

'Mr Bartlett . . .' said Gozo, his lip really trembling now.

'Then again, if we do get a ship for Gozo, the Gircassian Rift *is* on the way, isn't it, Jacques?'

Gozo looked quickly from Bartlett to Jacques and

back again. 'Is it? Is it?' he cried excitedly.

'Sort of,' said Bartlett, and they turned south, towards the sea, where it would be only a short journey—four weeks, or five, or six at the most—to the Gircassian Rift.

Gozo marched along excitedly. The idea of another adventure almost took away the disappointment of having missed the last one.

'What's in the book the Ahsap gave you, Mr Bartlett?' he said.

Bartlett stopped. He hadn't had time to look. Jacques and Gozo watched as he opened it and leafed through the pages. He grinned.

'It's the Ahsap's poems. Prule was right, Jacques— some of them really are quite silly . . . but . . . some of them . . .' Bartlett's voice trailed off to a murmur as he turned another page, '. . . some of them aren't.'

'What kind of a present is that?' cried Gozo. 'A book of silly poems!'

Bartlett closed the book and put it in his pocket. They started walking again. They left the dazzling white walls of the Pasha's city behind. Bartlett was thinking about the Ahsap, his slim face, his thoughtfulness, his search for ideas that would interest him. 'I think it's a very fine present,' he said eventually. He glanced at Jacques. Jacques, who had been thinking about it as well, nodded. 'I think there is probably nothing more important . . . more valuable to the Ahsap, that he could have given us.'

Gozo shrugged. 'Well, I suppose you did bring them

the sun. That's pretty valuable.'

Bartlett shook his head. 'We didn't bring them the sun, Gozo. We just helped them to see it.'

The Song of the Goat Stealers
(from the Ahsap's book of poems)

Under the moon, at the night time's noon,
We leave our tunnels behind.
We go rumbling free like a bumbling bee
Not knowing what we will find.
    (Not <u>knowing</u> what we will find!)

There's nothing so sweet as a goatified bleat
That floats on the sea of the night.
With a flop and a flip—like a fish with a ch'nip—
We go wriggling with delight.
    (We go <u>wriggling</u> with delight!)

For what's to be done we've no need of the sun—
The stars above are our lamps!
We follow the sound, and when they've been found,
We dance at the goatherds' camps.
    (We <u>dance</u> at the goatherds' camps!)

As they sleep their sleep—some shallow, some deep—
We swoop and swish round their tent.
And before they awake, their goaties we take,
And they'll never know where they went.
    (They'll <u>never</u> know where they went!)